OF THUNDER AND AMETHYST

THE WEATHER COURT GEM SERIES

KC SILVER

To those stepping into their power: don't be afraid to let go of what no longer serves you.

Note from the Author

Protecting your mental health matters. Please be mindful this book contains mentions of suicide.

One

Kamine adjusted her glasses as she craned her neck all the way back to get a good look at Skola—Thunder Court's school of Undertaking training. Its dominating presence was always a blemish on the horizon, towering in the center of the court. Who knew a large rock could be considered a school? The black exterior was as old as the land itself, but Kamine knew that the action happened inside the behemoth, where she would be forced to hone her magic in an effort to save her village during the yearly Undertaking; a time each year when rocks rained from the sky. It was a test from the Weather Gods for the people of the Thunder Court, and each year a new cohort entered Skola to prepare themselves to face that wrath.

Failure would lead to the court's downfall, their power dwindled and forever gone.

The first Undertaking Kamine could remember, she had spent under the bed. Her mother and father had tried coaxing her out, but she had refused to budge. Her parents had prepared her for what would happen, but at the time, it sounded like a story, not something that she would ever actually face. How could a child so young wrap their head around the fact that the world would one day come crumbling down on them?

"Be careful!" her father yelled, from behind her. She felt a slight push at her legs, as her little brother shoved her aside. Damien ran toward the stone structure with his arms extended and his hands desperate to explore. Small pebbles surrounded him, his powers manifesting effortlessly even at such a young age—a gift that he must have inherited from their mother. Damien didn't notice though, instead too curious about all the excitement around him. This was his first trip out of Polude, their village in the southern region of the Thunder Court. Her first time, too.

The court itself consisted of various rural villages and was situated between the Snow and Lightning Courts. It produced clay bricks that were imported to the other courts on the continent—including the Sun Court and Rain Court—and the bricks were traded with the Solar Courts across the sea. Most importantly, with the power that this court offered, many chose to leave and construct the actual building infrastructure with ease, but they were required to return each year for the Undertaking. They were not allowed to escape from the event, and if they dared try, it was said that the Weather Gods would curse them.

A sudden gust chilled Kamine's bones as she looked upon the various families in the square, clustered together. Parents were saying goodbye to their children, wishing them luck on a successful training, and later Undertaking. Kamine gulped down the tears threatening to spill as she watched a mother hug her daughter tightly.

She wouldn't allow herself to get emotional, not here, not for her deceased mother.

Kamine chased after her brother, grabbing him from under his arms to settle him on her hip. He had been seconds away from falling off the stone bridge that led to the entrance of the school. Just looking down at the abyss had been dizzying. She poked his small button nose, their mother's nose. "That's dangerous."

Damien only giggled, reaching to pull on her brown, curly hair. He barely understood his right from his left, so how could he comprehend the horror of what the school before them represented?

"He truly makes me appreciate how good you were as a kid." Her father relieved Damien from her arms and tickled under the boy's chin. "You'll cause quite the trouble, won't you?"

Let him, Kamine thought. Their lives had no guarantee. Their existences ran short—her mother being a perfect example. So let the kids have their fun, because once they turned twenty-two, they would be forever altered.

"They're going to call us in soon. You should go," Kamine said with little emotion in her voice. The faster they said their goodbyes, the better. Stalling wouldn't stop the inevitable.

Her father gave her a gentle smile as Damien stuck his tongue out at her. She hoped that after all of this, they were alive and well. She hoped that she would be able to come back home, and enjoy another meal with them by her side. Unfortunately, that future entirely depended on her ability to save them—an enormous hurdle she was about to face.

"You'll do great, Kamine," her father reassured her, his shaggy, brown hair blowing in the soft breeze. "These are the best teachers. They even trained me."

Kamine rolled her eyes, but appreciated the sentiment. She was just glad that he didn't bring up Mother. She wouldn't have been able to deal with that.

"I'll be okay," she nodded, acknowledging his comforting words, more for his sake than her own. Since she hadn't been able to access her powers, her father's worry was amplified. "I'm sure my cohort's professors will be knowledgeable and patient with me."

"Of course they will be. They only want to see you succeed."

As he put Damien down, she bent to the child's level and extended her hands. Damien ran into her arms. She cuddled him, kissing his cheek. "Be good for Father," she whispered. He shook his head. Truly a menace, that one.

Then she hugged her father, holding on just a moment longer than was necessary.

"Stay well," were his parting words, and Kamine turned around, grabbing her bag.

She took one last deep breath of fresh air before heading into the dark tunnels of Skola, hoping that the next time she walked across this bridge, it would be to save her family in the Undertaking.

Beyond the few sconces that lined the walls of the long hall-way—thanks to the Lightning Court—darkness took over. Already the space was too tight, the air too thick. The arched ceilings were not much taller than Kamine, and two bodies could barely fit side by side in the narrowness of the tunnel. It would be a long couple of months, simply trying to survive the day while her already light complexion turned gaunt.

She had no idea how she'd gotten into this mess.

Well...actually she did.

Her village voted her as this year's honored Undertaking participant. She had been placed on a ballot with all of her fellow villagers who had also turned twenty-two that year—the age that the Thunder Court deemed a person capable of having the lives of a whole village on their back. There was no choice to opt out, because the Weather Gods would surely damn the entire court if anyone tried. The winner represented their village, and with each village having its own representative, it amounted to a total of eight participants actively training their magic alongside one another. The Undertaking was a cruel test from the Weather Gods to prove that the people of the Thunder Court deserved their magic and deserved for those powers to be replenished yearly. Whoever was not cho-sen—aside from young children who had little concept or control of their magic—was banned from using their powers for the months before the Undertaking in order to preserve the realm's magic for the cohorts in training.

Kamine's village had chosen her.

It was her mother's fault, really. She had been a prodigy who not only saved her village with strength and pride, but who had also found the Heart in record time. The court treated the Undertaking like a massive game, and her mother had won it all. The shadow of her success clung to Kamine's shoulders like moss on a rock. The pressure of her mother's legacy was almost too much; Kamine wanted to turn around and run away from it all.

But the voices echoed from afar and the solidarity of the other student's shadows urged her onwards, further into Skola's dark underbelly.

Not wanting to stick out more than necessary, Kamine rushed to not be the last one to file inside. She followed the voices, making a sharp right turn and bumping directly into someone.

"Watch it!" the person grumbled, his voice deep and gravelly.

"Sorry," she responded, panic rising in her throat. Sconcelight illuminated his bearded face. He appeared her age, just much larger, with a bag slung over his shoulder, just like her. Another student then, she concluded. "Is that not where all the new cohorts are meeting?" Kamine pointed in the direction of the chatter.

The man scrunched his brows, inspecting her too closely for comfort. His eyes snagged at her fisted hands that trembled, then trailed upwards to meet her own gaze. His jaw tensed, likely noticing her purple eyes even in the dim light.

"Yes," he said, before heading off in the opposite direction of where everyone else was meeting.

Kamine shook off the strange interaction. She needed to focus. She couldn't worry about some guy not being able to follow basic directions.

She continued on until she reached a large room with a high ceiling. At the very top of the dome was a small hole that allowed sunlight to beam through. At least they weren't completely cut off from the world then.

Finding a spot in the back, Kamine rested against the rough stone wall, dropping her heavy bag at her feet. She had been so tense for days—*weeks*—leading up to this moment. Most nights, instead of sleeping, she wandered the forest not far from her home. She always felt connected to the ground, there, and what was buried beneath it. Without its comfort, she feared losing her sanity.

Someone stepped up beside her. "That outfit isn't going to do you any favors here." Kamine inspected what she wore—a simple ivory linen dress that reached her midcalf. "You stick out."

The woman speaking to her wore all black, with her pants and shirt clinging tight to her body, while her leather jacket hung loosely against her muscular frame. It was the conventional clothes of someone who would be training, something that protective gear could easily slip over with no fuss. Exactly why Kamine didn't want to wear it.

"The glasses are not a smart choice either."

Kamine huffed, tired of listening to this stranger's opinions. "I can't see otherwise."

"That honestly sounds like a blessing. This place is an eyesore."

"That's an understatement," she snorted. It was more than just an eyesore—it was a prison camouflaged as a school. "It's like I'm stuck inside a Weather God's asshole."

The woman's mouth dropped open, but she recovered with a big smile. Kamine tried not to cringe at the woman's sharpened teeth. She extended her hand, "I'm Janina."

"Kamine."

"I think we'll have some great fun together."

Kamine wasn't expecting that, but she'd take it. Anything to make her time here less miserable.

A woman at the front of the room clapped to draw the students' attention, her simple gray dress blending with the surroundings. She stood atop a platform, the sun shining directly on her like a spotlight. Everyone stopped their conversations to listen.

"I am Dritoria, the Headmaster of Skola. All of you have been chosen by your respective villages to represent them this year during the Undertaking. Your people have put immense trust in you. Now, it's time to prove yourself worthy. You have four months to sharpen your magic and skills, so when the time comes for it, you will be able to save your village with as few casualties as possible."

Kamine gulped, loathing this with every bit of her being. She fidgeted at the delicate golden bracelet at her wrist—a gift from her father to her mother after she had won the Undertaking. There should never be a single casualty in Kamine's opinion, but she wasn't one to talk. She had a lot of work ahead of her to make that as much of a reality as possible.

Headmaster Dritoria continued. "Of course, there is the Heart that one of you will find first, bringing your village the greatest honor. Once it is found, the Undertaking ends with our Goddess of Thunder giving mercy to the entire court. But it is said that all five Weather Gods will bestow great luck and prosperity on the individual who is the first to find the Heart. Last year's winner saw a surplus of potato growth in their village."

Each of the five Weather Courts were overseen by their own individual God, one that represented its power, but legend had it that all of them worked together to create the joint continent. Therefore, each court had an Undertaking that was unique to its governing God's will.

"However, heed my warning—if you try cheating your way through this, the Gods will punish you. Curse you." Headmaster Dritoria stared them all down with intense eyes that spoke of past experience of such occasions. "Winning the Heart is a privilege earned only by those who achieve it honorably."

The cohorts whispered amongst themselves. A voice that echoed across the room mentioned that two participants once fought each other for the Heart, pulling each other away from touching it. One of them was almost killed as a result. This was news to Kamine— she never kept up with the gossip surrounding the Undertakings.

"I'm bringing that shit home," Janina said, matter-of-factly, with no hesitation or doubt to be discerned in her voice.

Kamine gave her an encouraging nod. The last thing Kamine cared about was getting the Heart. She just wanted the people of her court to remain safe. That was her primary goal, and if her powers refused to present themselves, then she would need to find another way—no matter the cost.

Two

The Headmaster dismissed them to their rooms. She had announced that training would begin tomorrow morning, so the rest of their day could be used to get settled, and to explore the school halls. They were informed that training would occur daily, with no breaks. They only had a limited time, so the schedule would be intense and brutal, it seemed.

The curriculum was basic: cardio, muscle building, combat, and lastly, magic. She was not impressed by the curriculum and its lack of focus on the art of magic. Where were the history lessons, the strategy?

"I'm in Blue Hall, how about you?" Janina said.

Kamine flipped through her welcome packet and mumbled under her breath. "Purple Hall."

Janina quirked her mouth, pointing at Kamine's eyes. "That's fitting."

Kamine held back a groan. She didn't know how the cohorts had been sorted into their rooms, but she couldn't believe it was just a coincidence that she ended up where she did. Her purple eyes were a unique trait, one of the few things she had inherited from her mother.

"I don't even know where that is," Kamine muttered.

"I think the point is we figure this place out," Janina shrugged, brushing her fingers through her long black hair. "The faster we can navigate these endless halls, the better."

Kamine didn't question it. Of course the school would make a game of something as simple as finding where they'd be staying. One would think they would want the students focused on training or studying—not on navigating these old, dark halls.

"Want to grab dinner together later?" Janina asked, casually.

Kamine tried to not act stunned at the invite. In her village, people kept away from her, as if she was too sacred to be near. A descendant of such an honored winner, a legend, was too good for everyone else.

Feigning comfort, she shrugged, and replied, "Sure."

Janina left her, and the other participants began making their way to wherever the hell they would be sleeping for the next few months.

Kamine took one last moment to look up into the small hole in the ceiling to glimpse the sky above before she was locked away.

A soothing voice started from behind Kamine. "Your mother got so lost her first day, she ended up sleeping on the floor in here. When someone questioned her on it, she just said that she wanted to see the stars." The Headmaster laughed, her coiled, dark brown braids bouncing. "She was so prideful. Your father saw right through it. "

"Well, she lost that stubbornness after her Undertaking," Kamine snapped, tired of people speaking about the version of her mother that she never got to meet.

"We were all sorry to hear of her loss."

Kamine scoffed. She didn't need the Headmaster's sympathy. "I wasn't sorry. I'm glad she's no longer suffering."

Even though that wasn't entirely true. A deep part of her hated her mother for choosing to leave her and her family without so much as a goodbye letter. It was a selfish decision. A decision made out of guilt for her own actions. Yet, here Kamine was the one suffering for it.

Kamine stormed off with a quick farewell to the Headmaster, disappearing into the tunnels. She chose the direction that the mysterious man had gone earlier. Some internal instinct told her it was the right way, though there were no signs to guide her. She noticed other participants already running around the tunnels, exploring. Kamine just wanted to rest for the night.

Tomorrow everyone would learn how incapable she was, how her powers hid from her. It was a secret her mother had ruthlessly kept from everyone—a tactic that backfired, because the villagers now believed that Kamine would be their savior, that she had the same skill as her mother to protect them. And that couldn't have been farther from the truth.

In the distance, she spied a faint, purple glow. A breath of relief escaped her lips as she headed towards it.

Kamine startled back when she noticed a door swing open.

"You made it!" A voice said, cheerily.

A purple flame danced by the entryway. This must be Purple Hall, but there was only one room.

"I'm Zoya, your roommate." A tall, slim woman with two blonde braids said, as she extended her hand to Kamine. Her skirt and top looked to be hand knitted, the colors vibrant and the pattern chaotic. Her pale skin glowed purple in the light.

The room Kamine entered could barely be considered a closet. A bunk bed and a dresser—that's all that they were provided. Kamine's shoulders slumped.

"Where's the bathing room?"

Zoya's eyes widened. "I'm not sure. That's the next thing we need to find, I guess. It's likely a shared bathing room that we'll all need to use."

"Of course it is," she said under her breath. "I'm Kamine, by the way." She didn't want to start this out on the wrong foot. The one blessing of all this was that she no longer had to deal with a four-year-old boy barging into her room, and destroying it all.

"Oh I know," Zoya responded. At Kamine's scrunched brows, she added, with a smile on her face as if it were obvious, "We all know who you are."

"You do?"

"Everyone knows that your mother won her Undertaking." The unspoken words flitted in the air. *Everyone knows that your mother is the reason that the Thunder Court survived for another year.*

Just what she needed: everyone in her cohort to compare her to her mother.

Kamine put her bag down on the bottom bunk, since Zoya seemed to have claimed the top with colorful blankets. She would unpack later.

"I'm heading off for dinner, and to find the bathing room." She could use a hot meal, and a long bath.

"Oh," Zoya deflated, but recovered quickly. "Have fun."

Well, now Kamine felt bad for pushing her aside so quickly. It wasn't Zoya's fault. Kamine just didn't like the attention. "Want to come?"

Zoya nodded vigorously. They readied to leave, but as Kamine stepped out their small nook, she could have sworn she saw a shadow of a man pass by, with a familiar bag slung on his shoulder.

"This is more tragic than I could have expected," Janina whined dramatically from beside her, pushing the food around that she had only taken a few bites of. "Even in my poor village, we eat better than this."

Kamine and Zoya had bumped into Janina as they made their way over to the dining hall. Janina had been ranting about how confusing the tunnels were, and how she almost gave up and made residence in a small alcove. She also had been complaining about how hungry she was. Kamine's own stomach grumbled in response. She hadn't eaten this morning because of her nerves.

Unfortunately for them all, the dining hall was nothing to rave about. The chicken and vegetables were dry and flavorless. The cook had said something about food for fuel-over-flavor. Kamine had to chug the metal-tasting water just to be able to stomach it.

The other participants entered slowly, but no one sat at their table—something Kamine couldn't complain about. She didn't have the energy to engage with more people. To be fair though, the room was small enough that one could hear everyone's conversations, allowing her to at least gauge what this cohort would be like.

That's how she heard a petite but muscled man confidently utter to those at his table, "I can't wait to obliterate every falling rock." He demonstrated by taking the ceramic mug in his hands, throwing it, and crushing it midair with his powers as it came down.

As show-offish as that display was, it did reveal he was powerful. Most could only manipulate where rocks, stones, and clay moved. To break them like he did, they would need to smash it against something else. The fact he could make an object explode on its own without any outside forces advertised true skill. However, Kamine wondered if he could perform the trick on larger rocks, as that was what he'd be up against during the Undertaking.

A woman who sat next to him brushed off chunks of the shattered cup from her clothes, similar to those Janina wore. Her tight pink braid had been practically sealed to her scalp with wax, highlighting her high cheekbones and sharp jaw. "While you do that," her voice was cool and hard, "I'll be going for the Heart."

Kamine's ear perked at that. Others had joined in, nodding their heads. A few of them clanged their mugs of water together and cheered.

"Not with me stopping you," Janina mumbled from around the food in her mouth. A few pieces of chicken sputtered out as she spoke. Kamine tried not to cringe—not because of the chewed chicken that landed on her plate, but because Janina also was dead set on winning, like the others.

"Why do you care so much about the Heart?" Kamine asked, earnestly.

The room which had been noisy with the clatter of utensils and conversation came to a quiet pause. Kamine bit her bottom lip, immediately regretting asking her question so publicly.

"Because someone needs to find the Heart to ensure that power is restored, so why can't it be me?" The woman with pink hair pointed out.

Fair in a sense, she supposed, but that didn't get to the actual issue. "Will it matter that the power is back when all the people are dead because you cared more about glory than protecting them?"

"You underestimate me?"

Kamine could feel the growing tension in the room. She didn't need a fight breaking out. "I just think that those who are too focused on finding the Heart will fail to keep the people in their village safe."

Kamine and the woman stared intensely at each other. Although Kamine did not want to fight because she would be defenseless, she would not back down from her beliefs.

Zoya jumped in. "Have you heard there is a new magic professor?" All of the participants whipped their heads to Zoya. She shrunk at the attention, but kept going, "He's from my village in the east, Schod. Young and very handsome, if I remember correctly."

Someone else in the room snorted. "Yeah, I heard about him. I heard he's tough as hell."

"I heard that he won his Undertaking by literally tying down the other participants so he could reach the Heart first," another noted.

"Sounds hot," Janina said.

Kamine rolled her eyes.

"I also heard," Zoya added with a frightened demeanor, "that a beast roams these halls. One who lures you in, and does the God's bidding as it claws at your flesh."

"That's just an old tale to scare us into working hard," someone assured.

Zoya shrugged. "Perhaps, but it's still good to be cautious, especially when the tunnels are so unfamiliar, and it's easy to get lost."

Dread sliced through Kamine, and she could feel her face whiten. These revelations only confirmed what she had already known: the next few months would be pure torture.

Three

The first day of classes could not have been more brutal.

Kamine already sported bruises from combat class. The pink haired woman from dinner—who she now knew was named Roz—had not been gentle during sparring, when they were paired up. Apparently, she had been training for this from a young age. Her father had given her her first black eye, which she'd worn proudly. During their one-on-one practice, Roz got a few hard hits on Kamine before the professor pulled her back, preventing Roz from killing Kamine on the spot. Janina had laughed at Kamine's battered appearance, while her own lips were split, and stained with blood.

Even though they were allowed to wear protective armor during their Undertaking, the professor did not allow them to wear it during class. *A way to grow a hard shell*, she'd said. Hence, Kamine had been forced to wear a thin layer of clothes that were too tight on her body like the rest of the cohorts. The black material was foreign to her skin. She had to keep from constantly crossing her arms to cover herself. She already missed the flowingness of her usual linen dresses. She missed the outside air, too.

Now, they entered the classroom where they would learn how to perfect their magic, and make it more precise. At least, that's what the others would be doing. Kamine would just aim to do something, *anything*, with abilities meant to be innate, but for her were stubbornly withheld.

There was nowhere to even sit in the cavernous room. It was just a large room with a few rocks, ready to be manipulated. Kamine swallowed down her nerves. Perhaps she could hide in the back and avoid detection.

Janina and Zoya had given her curious looks all day, but did so especially now, as if they anticipated Kamine being so confident with her powers that she would want to show them off. She even heard rumblings from some of the cohorts that they were excited to see her in action—to see what the offspring of a previous Undertaking winner could do.

A tall figure walked through the door, his pace swift, but un-bothered by their presence. His hands were stuffed in the pockets of his black slacks, and he didn't even greet them before he started speaking.

"All of you in this room will fail your Undertaking," he said so simply, with little emotion or care. His white shirt was unbuttoned, and Kamine could just make out two black spots on his clavicle. It was a common tradition that Undertaking participants had stones lodged into their flesh as a reminder of what they had survived.

The man then stared right at her, and Kamine tried not to shrink back at the assessing gaze of his practically black eyes—like two orbs of darkness that could suck her into oblivion. He rubbed his beard, but stopped when he noticed his action.

Kamine recognized the man was the one she had bumped into when she had first arrived. His dark hair was pulled back loosely in a bun, and his rolled sleeves revealed his large, toned, veiny arms. He was a *professor*? Aside from his clothes, he looked like he belonged in the infantry, not here.

He paced the room, his hands behind his back. "None of you have the skills needed to save your village yet, which is why over the next few months, I, Professor Grimot, will break you and reform you into the winners you so desire to be."

Lycaster, whose shaved head had a large scar on it that strangely resembled a hawk, boasted, "My private tutors told me I'm good enough to win it all already."

Kamine prepared for the worst, but the professor didn't utter a response. No one in the room moved, the silence settling so deeply that Kamine could have sworn she heard the wind roaring from outside.

All of a sudden, a storm of small pebbles rocketed across the classroom, hitting them all. They ducked, covering their faces in an attempt to shield themselves. Someone whined about one rock hitting their eye. When Kamine unfurled herself from the danger, she saw how the strength of the professor's powers was enough to draw blood on herself and others.

The professor stepped up to Lycaster. "If you're so ready, why do you have cuts all over your skin? Someone who was truly skilled would have anticipated the attack, and would have been on the defensive."

Lycaster spit on the ground, while the professor smirked. Professor Grimot then addressed the whole class. "Anytime one of you speaks without permission, you will all be punished. I don't have time for childish behavior."

No one said a word, but they all got the message.

"Let's test your current abilities." He pulled out a piece of paper from his shirt pocket. He read it carefully, and Kamine knew the exact moment his eyes landed on her name.

"Kamine." The cohort parted, revealing her from the back. She supposed hiding wouldn't last forever. "Let's see if that magic from your mother was passed down."

Kamine opened her mouth to protest, but he stopped her. "I didn't give you permission to speak. Do you want more pebbles thrown at you?"

Kamine sullenly stalked to the center of the room. She flexed her hands as if that would finally help her powers come out, as if she hadn't tried that same tactic hundreds of times before.

He picked up a rock and tossed it to her like he would a ball. She at least caught it with her hands.

"This is magic class, not a game of fetch. I expect you to use your powers."

He picked up another and threw it harder this time. It hit her in the arm. She flinched slightly, but kept the reaction to a minimum.

"Again," he said, practically savoring her embarrassment. Her cheeks became rosier with each throw that she couldn't stop. He ambushed her with rocks that were bigger and thrown with more force. One hit her square in her chest. She stumbled slightly, needing to adjust her glasses as they slid down her nose. He hit her face right as she did, and the glasses fell to the ground. He was now just a blurry figure. Still, Kamine kept quiet, despite the panic rushing through her system. Her heart beat at a rapid pace, and she knew it wouldn't slow down unless she got out of this situation entirely.

"This isn't fair!" Janina shouted from the crowd.

Before anyone could blink, pebbles rained down on them all, again. Curses and yelling sounded from the cohort.

"I don't have time for amateurs who can't even stop a fucking rock from hitting them when they expect it. What are you going to do once you're in the Undertaking, and boulders are coming down at you and your village? What are you going to do when so many lives are at stake?"

Kamine didn't know. That was the problem. She had hoped one of her professors would be willing to discuss what her options would be. That seemed very unlikely now.

She couldn't see him very well, but she felt how his eyes were pinned on her.

"You aren't even trying, Kamine. At least do *something*," Professor Grimot hissed through his clenched teeth.

She bent down to pick up her glasses—which were mercifully not broken—and had only a second to put her arms out as another rock came her way. It scraped her skin hard enough that she felt a trickle of blood run down her forearm.

"Your hands are not going to be the answer."

Her eyes began to sting, but she fought to keep the tears back. They would not be productive.

"Can I have a break?" she whispered, as she grabbed for the bracelet that was hidden under the sleeve of her shirt.

"Breaks don't exist in the Undertaking."

She couldn't do this, but she was trapped with nowhere to go. She wouldn't run though. She refused to give him that satisfaction.

"Your mother must have been so ashamed when you inherited her eyes, but didn't get a lick of her abilities."

"Don't you dare—" More pebbles attacked them all before she could even finish.

Kamine could feel the other cohorts growing frustrated with her. Not at the person punishing them, but her—because of her incompetence.

"I'm done for today," she said with a little bite, her toughness gone now that he had taunted her about her mother. He had stepped past a line, into a space she didn't have the strength to follow him into. She went to the side with the others, accepting defeat. Janina tried to speak with her, but Kamine waved her into silence. She didn't want to cause any more trouble for them.

Professor Grimot had a satisfied air to him as he called up his next victim, one who performed much better than her. Kamine spent the rest of the class leaning on a hard, stone wall. Her injuries ached, and when she rolled up her sleeves, numerous bruises began blooming. Luckily, her bracelet was still intact. She anticipated that when one bruise faded, countless more would be added.

She had her work cut out for her.

"He's a sick bastard," Janina said from her spot on the couch. A bag of ice sitting on her shoulder matched that of Kamine's own.

They were resting in what they guessed to be a shared lounge for the whole cohort. There were a few plush couches, fur rugs, and soft blankets. Maybe the school took pity on the students, and provided at least this one source of comfort. Janina, Zoya, and Kamine felt fortunate to have found it. They were even luckier that none of the others had yet.

"He's a sadist," Zoya added. Surprisingly, she came out the most unscathed of the three of them. Her own skills during magic class showed there was a skilled fighter underneath her softness. "I'm sure you'll show him how great you actually really are. You were the tester today, but you'll be more prepared next time."

Kamine appreciated Zoya's optimism, but she figured it was finally time to reveal the truth that she held back for so long.

"I don't think so." They both straightened at that admission. "I have never been able to access my powers. I honestly don't know if they even exist." She wrung her hands together, touching the damned bracelet for comfort, but a sense of relief washed over her now that she had finally admitted her secret out loud.

"I don't understand—"

"I'm confused—"

They both started, simultaneously. Kamine couldn't blame them. She too would have a lot of questions. Hell, she *did* have a lot of questions.

"My powers haven't manifested. They never did when I was young, and they still haven't. I've been trying for years just to be able to push a small stone off the edge of a table." Kamine shrugged, ashamed at the truth. She remembered being a child, reduced to tears because of how badly she just wanted her magic to work. "I've never done it." But she knew they existed somewhere in the deep well of her soul because even if her magic has never physically revealed itself, once—so long ago—she felt a sudden spark within her. Since then, she had been chasing the same sensation, only to be met with failure.

Zoya ran her hand through her blonde hair, wavy from her braids, twisting it at the end around her finger. "But everyone has at least a little power in this court. Maybe you have used your powers, but it was just so small, it was hard to notice."

Janina added, "You must be doing something wrong."

Kamine rubbed her temple, the dim lights now less relaxing and more irritating to her vision. She could really use a breath of fresh air right now. "I promise, I've tried everything. The teas, the lessons, the research. All of it amounted to nothing."

"It's just," Janina interjected, "your mother was so skilled. There are tales of her being called a prodigy. Gifted with powers as great as the Weather Gods, from Buraza, herself."

Her mother's story was not a heroic tale, but a tragedy. The Thunder Goddess Buraza might have given her mother her powers, but Kamine had always described it as a curse, not a gift. Her mother's powers had a mind of their own, one her mother could never quell and control, especially after her Undertaking. Kamine feared Damien's powers would one day do the same, but if she thought of that too long, she worried she might actually claw her way out of here and run away with her brother to another court, so that he would never feel the pressure of their mother's past.

"Powers are not something we inherit. My mother's own parents had average skills," Kamine said.

Janina hummed, her melting bag of ice now forgotten on the floor. "Your mother found the Heart. I would think the Gods would honor that with strong offspring, which is why I still think there must be something great rumbling under your skin."

"You know," Zoya said with fervor. "My aunt also struggled for a long time. She was never chosen as a participant for the Undertaking, but she said that she would inflict pain unto herself, and that brought it out. Like her body subconsciously knew that pain meant danger, and danger meant needing to protect herself."

"That sounds uncomfortable." Kamine tightened her lips. "Plus that was exactly what happened this afternoon in magic class. The pain didn't do anything."

Zoya thought about it for a second, then responded. "Perhaps because it wasn't danger that you felt, but embarrassment. Your life wasn't being threatened, just your pride."

"It felt like I might die."

Janina laughed. "But deep down you knew you wouldn't, because Professor Grimot would have gotten in big trouble."

Kamine didn't know if she believed that. He seemed to be the person to take things too far, his emotions uncontrolled. But...he had won his Undertaking for a reason, so he clearly had a lot to teach that could be beneficial to her. First though, she would need to get her powers to wake up.

"So we test this theory then." Kamine said, finally. She would do anything to prepare herself for the Undertaking—anything to keep her villagers alive. "But what, exactly?"

"Maybe we drown you?" Janina offered.

"*What*?" She couldn't be serious.

"We can turn one of the baths into an ice bath, and force you to stay under."

Zoya nodded. "That might work."

"That sounds dangerous."

Janina smiled, her teeth still stained with blood from earlier. "Perfect."

Grimot leaned back on the creaky chair in the empty office. Headmaster Dritoria had one of her lackeys deliver a note to his private room less than hour ago, demanding his presence immediately. Before trekking his way over, he decided to finish off the chapter of his book. He walked slowly to delay his arrival time and was unsurprised to find the Headmaster was not there.

He would give her an extra minute before leaving. Inspecting the clock on the wooden desk, he willed the second hand to move faster. He had a nice drink of alcohol waiting for him back in his room. The first day of class, and already he wanted this to end. The entire cohort was useless. Only Roz and Franciz had shown some promise. Franciz's small stature and strong powers would benefit him greatly, while Roz's determination would get her far.

He uncrossed his legs and stood. As soon as he turned to face the door, though, it opened and the Headmaster stepped in. Her dark skin was illuminated by the warm lights surrounding them.

"Please sit," she said simply, but there was an underlying authority to it that made him slouch back into the uncomfortable chair.

Headmaster Dritoria had hated Grimot since the day he had walked into this school as a cohort member, ready to face his Undertaking. She took one look at him during that first day, sighed exasperatedly, and had been up his ass ever since. It might have had to do with the fact that he used his powers to block various hallways with large rocks throughout the school, creating mass confusion when no other students could find their rooms. Could one really blame him? The school encouraged competition, and he liked winning.

That was the reason he had done everything to win his Undertaking, and why he needed his students to succeed. Not only would failing cause the destruction in a village, but it would harm his chances of breaking the curse now bestowed upon him from the Gods. No one could fall behind—which made Kamine a huge problem.

Headmaster Dritoria relaxed in her chair and steepled her hands together. He could hear her tapping her feet.

"I know you know why you're here," she said.

Grimot tried not to roll his eyes. "Does it have to do with a student who can't even defend themselves against a pebble?"

"No, it has to do with *you* physically assaulting a student," she said angrily, not taking his shit.

He huffed a laugh. Unbelievable that such an accusation was being thrown at him. "That's a stretch. It's class. A demonstration."

She shook her head. "I didn't hear about any teaching happening."

"And who exactly did you hear this from?" He would make sure they suffered.

The Headmaster cocked her head to the right. "I have ears all over this school, don't try to test me."

Grimot narrowed his eyes, but said, "My methods are harsh, but effective. A necessity to get them into shape by the Undertaking."

"What you need is a full cohort to participate. If one of them is killed on your watch, then you'll be the one a village comes after when there is no one there defending them. And I won't help bail you out."

She had a point. As much as he wanted to destroy these students' spirits, the court needed them alive for the Undertaking.

"I'll be gentler," he promised.

"Gentler, *and* you need to apologize to the student." He opened his mouth to protest, but she stopped him. "No excuses. You are not a child, so I do not want to hear your complaints. I hired you because of your skill. Don't make me regret it." She said, sternly. "Now, leave." She pointed to the door. "If I catch wind of something like this again, I will dismiss you without hesitation."

If Grimot was out of this job, then he could never prove himself to the Gods. His curse would doom him to a fate worse than death. Damn him; but he couldn't let that happen.

Four

After another day of grueling classes, Kamine, Janina, and Zoya were now all in the bathing room in the middle of the night. The large room was quiet, except for the stream of water coming from the small waterfall, filling the bath. Steam effused the strong scent of herbs, and the other baths were thankfully empty, though the girls had chosen the late hour to avoid an audience. It was almost peaceful, but knowing what came next left Kamine's heart pounding in her ears. She did not want any witnesses to what would surely be a sad spectacle.

The other cohort members had already started making jokes about her lack of powers by hiding their faces with their hands, just like she had done when the rocks were thrown at her. She was just grateful that magic class was not scheduled everyday, because otherwise she would never have a moment to recover. They had engaged in cardio and muscle building today, and thankfully she had been the fastest runner. However, it was a skill that wouldn't help her all that much during the Undertaking—but at least she was mildly capable of doing something right.

"I think this is a bad idea." Zoya said from the corner, her arms wrapped around her knees. She was wearing another bright colored ensemble made by her own hands—as were all her clothes—Kamine had been told when she asked about them.

"You say that *now*?" The bottom half of Kamine's body already sat at a ledge inside the large hole in the ground that the school considered a bath. Her toes didn't reach the ground when she stood, the depth expansive and unknowable.

They all had to drag in bags of ice from the kitchens. The cooks had not been impressed when they had asked for them. Kamine just hoped it was enough to have an impact.

"It's not a bad idea, it's brilliant." Janina corrected as she dumped the first bag. The ice bounced up and floated. "This will work."

"I wouldn't be so confident," Kamine responded.

"Well, this could go quicker if Zoya helped." Janina said pointedly to the woman who still had not moved from her spot. Zoya startled at being called out and grabbed her own bag.

The water began to cool down. It wasn't unbearable yet, but Kamine guessed it would soon turn tortuous. She had worn her full training clothes to keep her warm for as long as possible.

"Last one," Janina announced, pouring the ice from high up, which caused it to cascade down Kamine's arms.

"Ouch," Kamine yelped. "I don't need you adding to my growing collection of bruises."

"Sorry," she winced.

Kamine waved her off, not actually in that much pain. "So the plan is that you'll hold my head down, and if I'm literally on the brink of passing out, I'll start kicking or waving my arms around for you to stop, right?"

They both nodded.

"You got this," Zoya encouraged, even though her face showcased her own fear.

Kamine passed along her glasses to Zoya and took one last deep breath, savoring her life, before dipping her head under the freezing water.

She opened her eyes immediately, needing to know her surroundings. It was practically pitch black, but she could see the outline of her hands if she brought them close to her face. She looked at her palms, and willed them to do something. Janina and Zoya left a pile of small rocks for her outside the bath to manipulate. She just had to move one rock, and they would let her up. Simple, so simple. Even her four-year-old brother would be able to do it.

She flexed and unflexed her hands. She thought about the rocks moving, and envisioned them flying across the room, and splashing into another bath.

Only shards of ice responded, burning her skin as they floated in the cold bath. She shook her head, focusing again.

Move, move, move, she repeated like a mantra.

She thought of her mother who failed, her mother who let her own selfishness get in the way of acting as a parent. The moment she discovered her mother dead had stuck with Kamine like a splinter that refused to budge no matter how much she tried to pick it out.

She couldn't breathe.

Panic set in as her lungs began to burn. Her mouth begged to open and let in some air, but she forced it closed. There was no air here. Only water, all water.

She used that fear to call to her powers. *Work you blasted, useless thing. Save me.*

But no one pulled her back up. She hadn't successfully used her powers, then.

Kamine was growing desperate, her mind no longer centered on her powers, but rather on the growing need to get the fuck out of the cold water. A thought passed her that she would die. Right there, right then. Maybe that would be for the best. That way, she would never have to face the Undertaking, never have to face her failure, and never become a hollow shell like her mother had become.

But, if that happened, then her whole village would die.

Kamine cried out, water funneling down her throat. Her body ached, her limbs frozen. Kamine fell deeper and deeper into a pit of cold darkness. This was it. She couldn't tell up from down anymore. It didn't matter.

Something warm swam by her. Something moved. She didn't react, however, nor feel scared. Let the creature eat her. Let it relieve her despair.

It grabbed her and lifted her up, up, up—until she gasped as she broke the surface of the water.

"You idiots!" a male voice yelled. The presence forced her down onto her back and pumped at her chest. As she coughed, and heaved, and vomited all over herself, she didn't have it in her to be embarrassed.

She could hear an intake of breath from somewhere near. Zoya, she thought through the fog as she came back to her senses. Her body shivered, and her hair clung to her face, cold water dripped down her skin, onto the tiled stone.

"What the hell were you doing?" the man asked her. But even if her frozen lips could muster a word, her mind was incapable of constructing a coherent sentence.

Thankfully, Janina responded, her voice a whisper. "We were trying to help. We thought it would nudge her powers."

"What idiots would think that would work?" He gritted. As he held Kamine, he shook her like he needed to physically relieve his growing frustration.

For some reason, that angered Kamine. This man had no right to reprimand her friends for trying to help. Because that is what they had become even in such a short time. Her friends—who didn't judge her for her lack of powers, and who only wanted to help her reach her potential.

Kamine finally opened her eyes, and registered exactly who it was. She narrowed her eyes at Professor Grimot. "Get away from me!" She weakly shoved him back from her, the stones on his clavicle poking at her skin. "Don't you dare touch me without my permission."

His usual lightly-tanned face looked practically ashen, and his shoulder-length black hair was a soggy mess.

"You were seconds away from dying, and you're angry that I touched you so I could save you?" He sounded exasperated, his tone condescending.

Janina stepped in, kneeling beside Kamine and sliding her glasses back on. With Kamine's vision no longer blurry, she could see everyone's reactions clearly now. Janina looked disturbed by the whole scene, but she brushed Kamine's hair from her eyes. "I think she might just be in shock."

"No." Kamine said clearly. "I don't want him anywhere near me."

He squeezed the bottom of his shirt, water trickling down. He was avoiding her gaze, or he just didn't care. What Kamine didn't expect was to see the outline of his torso through his damp shirt. His muscles rippled under the see-through fabric, his long torso beautifully formed, with a sprinkle of dark hair that covered it. She didn't allow herself to stare too long.

"You'll be stuck with me for the next few months. You can't get rid of me that easily, *Kammy*."

"Kamine," she corrected, her eyes hard as stone. "And what were you even doing in here?"

He rolled his eyes. "Contrary to what you might think, the whole school shares this bathing room. Even professors need to clean up after a long day."

Oh, Kamine thought. She supposed that was a simple enough explanation, even if the late hour suggested that sleep eluded him like it did her.

"Go to bed," he ordered. "All of you."

Zoya unraveled her body from the small ball she had been in. She was shaking, and Kamine felt guilty for scaring her.

Janina and Zoya helped her up unto unsteady legs.

"Do you think you can walk back to your room?" Janina asked.

Professor Grimot remained kneeling, still looking down at the ground. It was as if he was waiting for her to answer, waiting to hear if he would need to assist her to her room.

"I'm fine," she choked out, her voice raw.

Kamine used both her friends as support, wrapping her arms around their shoulders as she walked off the ordeal. She would surely regret this during class tomorrow, where she could almost guarantee Professor Grimot would punish her for taking such a foolish risk.

Five

Grimot would kill her, if she didn't kill herself first. If she really cared so little about her own life, then he would remind her exactly why dying was a coward's move.

He stormed into the classroom, and abruptly halted when he saw Headmaster Dritoria. She was leaning against the wall, chatting with some of the students. Her hands moved animatedly as if she were telling a great story on a stage, instead of being encased in a large hole in a mountain with no sun. He may have his own personal issues with her, but she was clearly a good leader who was passionate about her role.

"Professor Grimot," she smiled when she noticed him. "I'm excited to observe the students today. See where they are starting from, and how they'll improve under your care."

"Wonderful," he mumbled under his breath. He dreaded the next two hours.

"I think there is something you need to say before class begins, correct?" Her high, joyous pitch grated his ears.

Grimot internally groaned. Maybe he should just off *himself* at this point. Maybe he understood why Kamine wanted to do it, especially with how he had embarrassed her.

He faced the poor victim. She was dressed in Skola training clothes, the black fabric hugging her body like a second skin. He could tell she hated wearing it, with the way she stood with her shoulders slumped. He agreed that it didn't suit her. He preferred the dress she had been wearing the first day, when she bumped into him. He thought of the way the fabric billowed behind her, the white contrasting against the stark darkness of their environment. It suited her.

Expectant eyes stared at him.

He cleared his throat. "I may have overstepped during our first class, and taken things too far, too quickly. After all, I expected greatness from such inexperienced children." Someone in the room snorted.

"We're adults, jackass," someone else said. Grimot guessed it was Lycaster. He hadn't learned from their first lesson that outbursts were not tolerated. Perhaps he could loosen up his teaching style, just slightly, so that he wouldn't have the Headmaster constantly disturbing their precious time.

Headmaster Dritoria butted in. "I think there is someone specific that this should be directed towards."

Right, Kamine. She wasn't even looking at him, instead she was reading a worn book that looked about ready to crumble into dust.

Her eyes moved quickly across the page, her one hand playing with something at her wrist.

Through gritted teeth, he said, "My apologies to Kamine."

She ignored him, her eyes still focused on the page. Headmaster Dritoria softly cleared her throat to try to get Kamine's attention, but the Headmaster had more patience than he did.

"Did you hear me?" he said, a little louder.

Kamine finally turned her attention to him, slamming the book shut. "I did. I don't accept."

"Don't accept what?"

"The apology."

So much for taking it easier. He stalked over to her, ripped the book from her hands, and threw it across the room. "You don't get to decide whether to accept or not."

"Actually, that's exactly how apologies work. But I'm not surprised that someone like you doesn't understand that basic etiquette."

His jaw tightened as his hands cinched into fists.

Headmaster Dritoria clapped, her authority causing some rocks from the ceiling to crumble and fall. "Kamine, Professor Grimot is sincerely sorry for his behavior in the last class. Please accept his apology so that class can resume."

For the second time in his life, he was grateful for the woman. The first had been when she had allowed him to become a professor.

Kamine pushed up her glasses. "Fine."

"Great," Headmaster Dritoria said. "Now that that's sorted, I'm going to let you begin your lesson." She then excused herself, her rose scented perfume wafting across the room.

So she hadn't actually cared about the progress of the students—or at least she had a second motive. She wanted to keep an eye on him as if he were a child, as if the apology itself wasn't embarrassing enough.

Grimot stood at the front of the classroom. "We'll be doing the same exercise. You—" he pointed to Lycaster, whose powers needed a lot of work. "You're first."

Kamine sat cross legged on the ground. When she did, she knew that Professor Grimot clocked it, and that he desperately wanted to reprimand her. For some reason, he held back. In fact, he completely ignored her. Everyone was called one by one to the front of the classroom to try and defend themselves from an oncoming rock. Some even moved onto larger boulders, including Janina and Zoya.

With the way it was going, Kamine would be last.

At least that gave her an opportunity to observe, to closely examine the tactics that she needed to try. Most of the cohorts moved their hands, which allowed them to redirect the trajectory of the rock. Others, like Franciz, could destroy the rock while it was mid air. He seemed to flinch his neck slightly, to do that. One student—Magda—even resorted to kicking the rocks with their heavy boots. Professor Grimot did not like that, proven by how he threw a larger rock the next time. They were now in the infirmary with a broken toe, most likely.

Kamine waited and waited, anticipating her turn.

But it never came.

"Class is over," Professor Grimot said. "Next time, we'll move on to have multiple objects being thrown at you at once."

The students began to file out of the classroom. Janina and Zoya both bit their lips, clearly noticing Kamine's lack of a turn.

"Go ahead," Kamine said, stretching her legs. They had grown stiff after she had sat for nearly two hours. "I'll catch up with you later."

They nodded nervously. Zoya even rubbed Kamine's shoulder, and wished her good luck.

Professor Grimot used his powers to move all the rocks back into neat piles. He could lift many at once, with not a grimace of discomfort. Kamine dreamed of the day she could move just one with such ease.

"Professor," she said. He turned towards her, his eyes widening, as if finally noticing that everyone else had left, perhaps even confused why she was still here. "Do you have a moment?"

Kamine could tell he had the urge to say no, but she continued on before he could reject her. "I was wondering why I didn't have a chance to practice today." She tried to sound innocent, not angry. She didn't need his hostility, or to fuel his hatred of her.

A rock floated above her head, and she winced when it grazed her curly hair.

"You clearly don't take this seriously, so why should I waste my time."

"I spent last night torturing myself to try and trigger my powers. Is that not serious enough for you?"

"Thinking that inflicting pain will make your powers come out is stupid, and naïve."

Her mouth gaped open. It was unbelievable that he thought so little of her. "I have read numerous accounts from past Undertaking participants that their powers amplified during it because of their fear. It was not crazy to try something so extreme." She crossed her arms, her point made.

He just laughed—actually laughed—his shoulder-length, wavy hair shaking as he did. "Reading is not going to solve your problem."

"Problem?"

"Something is holding your powers back, and the only person who can unearth that is you."

"So, what, I'm supposed to just practice by myself with zero guidance for the next few months? Do you not think that is what I spent my whole life doing?"

"Not by yourself. With me."

What was this man saying? "That is the point of this class! Yet, you ignored me."

"Not during class," he clarified. "Just you and me."

She blinked, stunned by the offer. "Is this approved by the Headmaster?"

"I don't need her approval."

Kamine prepared to retort, but she stopped herself, and thought about it. Private lessons might actually be the solution.

"I could see you thinking, Kammy—"

"Kamine."

"Accept. Or face the reality that your village might be left in ruin."

"You're so confident in yourself, aren't you?"

He lifted a heavy rock using his hands, his arms straining against his white shirt. Kamine ignored his corded forearms with little success. He extended the rock, offering it to her. Kamine put her arms out, and he dropped it into her grasp. She fell immediately to the ground, the rock almost crushing her hands completely before she could swipe them from under it at the last moment.

"You're desperate, and that makes you willing to try anything."

Kamine didn't like the sound of that. But he was right, and she hated it. She could always back out if it wasn't working, right?

"Fine," she said. "When do we begin?"

Six

Grimot could not believe what he agreed to, could not believe that he offered more of his precious time away. Not to just anyone, but to a student that was clearly hopeless, who didn't seem to have an ounce of magic running through her veins. The only positive was that Kamine seemed determined to do anything. And what choice did he have? If even one of his students failed, then his curse would come to fruition.

"You look angry, Grim," a voice he recognized all too well said. Kestra spit out a cherry pit into a bowl as she stared at him, pity in her eyes. "Tough first week?"

Kestra was Headmaster Dritoria's right hand. She worked through all the logistics of class schedules, boarding rooms, and everything in between. Most importantly, she was gifted with the sight of the Weather Gods. She was the agent that followed whatever dreams the Gods bestowed on her. She would be the one to place the Heart where the Gods wished it. That meant she knew everything. Even information Headmaster Dritoria was not privy to.

But Kestra was the reason he was in this predicament.

Grimot wanted to turn back around and avoid her, but that would be running away, and he refused to be spineless. He stepped into the room.

"You look bored. Haven't found a new student to harass yet?"

She smiled, her white teeth gleaming even in the dim, cavernous room. "I always appreciate how you're never afraid to be a bitch to people. Even when you were a student, you never backed down."

"That's how you win."

"Well, I wouldn't go that far," Kestra said, a little too proudly. "I helped you win, remember?"

Of course she had to remind him. She loved bringing it up at every opportunity. Unfortunately for him, she was right. Her insider information had allowed him to find the Heart in record time, even beating Kamine's mother's timing. As a result, the Gods had christened him a cheater.

"Your guidance only got me so far," he clarified. "That information would be pointless in the hands of someone powerless." A weak excuse, but he needed to gain higher ground with her.

She sighed deeply and got up from her seat to place her hands on both his shoulders. She squeezed gently. Her nails were painted bright pink, a color she never strayed from. Those exact fingers, with that exact color, once wrapped around his length, stroking him. He shuddered at the memory.

"No need to get defensive. It's all in the past now."

He wished it was, but he could read it on her face that she expected more from him. She had kept their secret because it would equally hurt her reputation. He anticipated that one day, she would fuck all, and let everyone know that he was a fraud—that he had used his body to seduce, and tempt the words of where the Heart would be located from her mouth. How his tongue had trailed from her clit, upwards, to her neck, as if dragging the truth out of her with each and every one of her breathy moans. It had worked, and at the time, he'd had no regrets. Even months after winning, the glory and fame had seemed worth it.

That all changed when the reality of his Undertaking hit him like one of those boulders, and his mind and body could no longer function with his deceit coursing through him. Then, Kestra revealed what she had seen in a dream, how all five Weather Gods had appeared to her and damned him. They would punish him if he didn't show his dedication to the court by teaching this cohort until they succeeded, with no cheating involved. Failure would lead him to turn to stone, while his mind remained completely conscious of his surroundings.

A curse.

After he won, he had become directionless and unmotivated. His one purpose in life was now gone, wiped away as soon as his hands touched the amethyst gem that was this court's Heart. Now, his only goal was to continue living and living better, even if he already had suffered signs of his body changing. Every day he woke up more stiff than the last, his joints less flexible, as if they were being crusted over with dried clay.

"Right," he said, removing her arms from around him. "Let's keep it in the past, then."

She pouted, her pursed lips so close to his. "But I miss this." She placed her hands on his pants, right over his cock, but he refused to be affected by it. She rubbed him, and he closed his eyes, breathing through it. "You certainly have gotten pickier. This used to wind you up so fast."

"I was younger, and far more stupid then."

"Oh please," she turned around, swaying her hips as she picked another cherry and popped it into her mouth. Having been a student before, Grimot knew that the school spoiled the professors when it came to food. Grimot remembered having to stomach the most awful mush. He would have to drink water with each spoonful just to get it down. Many had rumored that the food contained a powder sourced from the Weather Gods that would energize the students. Some said that it was amethyst—the same gemstone as the Heart—ground into dust. Grimot never really cared. "That was only five years ago. You're still young. Much younger than me at least."

She had been minister for many years already when Grimot arrived as a participant. Now, she was somewhere in her mid-forties, in comparison to Grimot's twenty-seven. Still, an Undertaking changed a person. It was one thing to just live through the yearly Undertaking as a bystander, and another to be the one that determined the fate of a village's survival.

"I have somewhere to be."

"Running away so quickly?" she chuckled, the sound chasing him as he sought the privacy of his room.

"I can't believe what I agreed to," Kamine whined to her friends, as she laid on her bunk. She stared up at the bottom of the top bunk that she could touch with her hands. She had already hit her head on it this morning when she woke up. "I'm an idiot, a masochist."

Her friends weren't saying anything, just letting her vent. Zoya and Janina tossed a rock back and forth to each other with their powers. With each throw, they made the rock do flips and tricks in the air. At one point, Zoya bounced the rock off Kamine's knee.

"Tell me how to get out of this," Kamine begged. She had to find a solution. Perhaps she could go to Headmaster Dritoria and claim that Professor Grimot forced her into the agreement. But that would be a lie, and she didn't want to outcast herself further.

"Maybe just don't show up," Janina offered from her spot on top of the dresser. She sat with her legs crossed, the wood groaning under her weight. Even the furniture here was barely functional.

"That sounds like a dumb plan," Kamine said, exasperated. She just wanted to close her eyes and sleep, but how could she when tomorrow, she would be spending private time with a man who clearly had it out for her. When they had arrived at the Purple Hall, there was a note waiting there for Kamine, letting her know the time to meet Professor Grimot in the magic classroom.

"I think this will be a good thing. Practicing without an audience of judging eyes might allow you to relax."

Of course Zoya would see the positive here. Kamine wished she could see it the same way. Instead, she expected to leave the session with tears streaking her face as she limped through the halls.

Janina jumped down from her spot, threw the rock outside the door, and waited. Within seconds, the rock came back like a boomerang. "It's better than what we've tried."

"Also, just think. The others are going to be so jealous that you get extra time with him. That alone should feel satisfying. I know Roz would beg on her knees for it."

Kamine turned to her side, looking up at the both of them. "I guess you're right."

Janina stretched her back. "Speaking of Roz, I should head back to my room. She'll get pissed if I disturb her beauty sleep, and I don't want to wake up tomorrow buried in rocks."

Zoya raised her brows. "Did she threaten to do that?"

"No, but her eyes tell all."

"I fucking hate this place," Kamine admitted.

"Well, we're stuck, so let's make the best of it."

Janina nodded at Zoya's words. "Who knows, after all the training with Professor Grimot, you might even be the one to find the Heart."

Kamine gasped dramatically. "Janina, thinking of the possibility of someone else getting the Heart? You must have hit your head."

"It might be possible," Janina started, "only if I were dead before I could get there first."

Seven

Grimot walked into the magic classroom as Kamine was bent over, stretching. Her hands touched the ground easily from the looks of it, her palms flat on the surface. She didn't seem to hear him come in.

It was strange to be in this classroom again, now as a professor. He loved being a student, and showing off skills to the others. He and Kestra would also fuck in here often, the large empty room providing a pleasant echo chamber for their moans. It was a room that had boosted his ego those years ago, but now it just looked sad and lonely. Even the glittering chandelier that hung high up in the vaulted ceiling—a hazard if he were honest, but a thought he kept to himself—couldn't elevate his perception of the room again.

He cleared his throat, and Kamine whipped up from her position. Her glasses slipped down her nose, and she adjusted them as her face turned a slight tinge of red, likely more out of the sudden redistribution of her blood flow than embarrassment.

"Stand over there," he commanded, pointing to the center of the room.

"Good morning to you, too," she mumbled, but did as she was told.

Her curly hair was pulled back, but wisps of it sprung out, and he could practically see the nerves on her face. The way she bit her bottom lip and furrowed her brows. The way she kept fidgeting with whatever was hidden on her wrist, or her glasses, as if she prepared for them to fly off her face any moment.

He came towards her with a rock in his hand. She tensed, and he *almost* felt guilty for making her so scared of him—for having her think that his presence meant harm. Then, he remembered that the Undertaking was a brutal bitch, and that boulders raining from the sky would be destroying her village without any care for her feelings.

Plus, his life, too, was on the line. Being a jerk was warranted, in his opinion.

He stood a few feet away from her, close enough to touch her if he outstretched his arms, but he kept his hands to himself. Her eyes were on the rock. Either she was trying to will it to move, or she was avoiding eye contact with him.

He bent down and placed the rock in front of her feet.

"First lesson," he said. "Instead of stopping a rock in midair, I want you to lift the rock into your hands." Satisfied with himself, he took a seat at the far end of the room and picked up the book he brought with him.

"That's it?" she asked in disbelief. "No words of advice?"

He ignored her. The more time they spoke, the less time she spent practicing. Also, he found that he liked riling her up.

She cracked her neck, the loud pops traveling to his ears.

He didn't watch her, but the shadows on the wall revealed that she moved her hands. It was like she hoped to create a gust of wind strong enough to lift the rock. She made circles over, and over again, but nothing happened. Of course it didn't. Shortly after, he could hear her pacing, like she was staring down a frightened animal.

Her frustration grew as she swore under her breath, her mouth absolutely filthy. He hated that he liked how it sounded. The words were enunciated, the exasperation at herself echoing off each wall, each reverberation a sound of defeat. He could tell this wasn't her first time attempting to bring her powers out, and failing. She was well versed in disappointment.

He still wouldn't give her the relief of stepping in. Not yet. She needed to be reminded of exactly what she thought would work, so she knew exactly what she did wrong. At this moment in time, she was a failure—one who still had to prove herself. But if she could fix this, then maybe he, too, wouldn't be a failure in the eyes of the Gods anymore, and he could come out of this with his limbs still made of flesh and bone.

Kamine curled the metal bar towards her chest. The weight of it burned her arms, but at least she felt something, at least her body could do *something*.

Her head, on the other hand, pounded. Her lesson with Professor Grimot was a disaster. He didn't provide any words of advice, and she refused to beg him for any. She wouldn't let him see her as more of a weakling than he likely already did.

Kamine followed her usual routine for trying to make her magic obey. Every time she tried to use her powers, she would move her arms, say words, and strain her mind. She even twitched her neck like Franciz had done during class. But none of it worked.

Roz grunted. Her pink hair was tightly coiled into a large mass on top of her head, not a single strand of hair out of place. "Are you trying to get private weight lifting lessons, too?" Roz asked, as she gritted her teeth. She lifted a large rock above her head, held it, and dropped it. Being in a large mountain, one could barely feel the impact of it.

"Pardon?"

Roz wiped her nose, her face flushed. "I just noticed that you barely carry anything of substantial weight. I was just wondering if that was on purpose. Are you trying to get more alone time with the professors?"

Kamine frowned. "Of course not. I just have weak arms."

Roz grumbled, "Of course, that's it."

Janina and Zoya were both in a corner spotting each other as they took turns lifting the weights. Kamine could hear that they stopped and watched her now, ready to jump in as needed.

"I'm confused why you care so much," Kamine said, careful to not be too loud so that the rest of the cohort couldn't hear their conversation. Professor Sandomir was preoccupied with another student, fixing their form. "I would think you'd be glad I'm so bad at this. It's one less person to compete against for the Heart."

Because to all them, that's what mattered. Even if Kamine were strong and powerful, she still would have different priorities. Her father's and brother's lives being the most important ones.

"I would just think that the offspring of an Undertaking winner would be preparing their whole life for this, that they'd be the best. It seems like you never cared to bother, even though it would be obvious to anyone that you'd be voted as your village's participant when you came of age."

Roz's patronizing tone wouldn't give her what she desired: a fight.

Kamine shrugged. She was rolling the metal bar with her feet, the movement methodical. The exact thing she needed to keep calm. "Who's to say I don't have other methods of protecting my village?"

"We all know nothing else will work besides using your powers to stop the boulders from falling down. Other methods have only led to more deaths."

Roz was right. There were accounts of participants hiding villagers in shelters made of rock. Unfortunately, a large boulder always seemed to fall on it. The structure crumbled and all under it had died, because the Gods considered it cheating.

"Yet you'll likely be running straight for the Heart instead of helping your own village," Kamine shot back.

As the years went on and the Undertaking had become more of a competition than a test one worked to pass, participants had been more likely to ignore the plight of their villages. Kamine had been witness to it. A few years ago—thankfully, before Damien was born—their village's participant was nowhere to be found during the Undertaking. As bystanders, villagers couldn't use their powers to save themselves. Granted, they had limited powers left at that point as the court was practically depleted of it, so the only way not to die was to dodge the oncoming storm of rocks. It was scary as fuck, and even scarier when you had a mother who showed no emotions as the storm of rocks raged, a mother who would try to escape the house to be outside in the storm. Kamine's father had to carry her back inside to keep her safe.

Professor Sandomir approached them both.

"This isn't a gossip session. Get to lifting," he said, then started yelling at a group who were seconds away from seriously hurting themselves by showing off.

Kamine bent down and picked up the metal bar again. Her hand was cramping from all the lifting, but she wouldn't allow herself to complain.

"I would never leave my village to fend for itself," Roz whispered to Kamine as she laid back on a bench. "I want my family and neighbors alive more than anything. *More* than the Heart, even." Then, her sad face became neutral again. "I just think I have the ability to do both, because I'm that good." Roz grabbed the bar above her head, adjusting her grip. "Now, spot me, weakling. I know you're stronger than you let on."

Kamine couldn't help it, a smile crossed her face.

Eight

Yet again, Professor Grimot completely ignored Kamine during their lesson, reading his book, and writing notes within it, instead. She at least hoped that he was reading something interesting. Perhaps he was learning new ways to torture students without getting blood on his hands. She could imagine him back in his room, testing out how long he could place a large rock on a person's chest before it would suffocate them, or maybe, a way to force pebbles down someone's throat, choking them.

"I didn't tell you to stop."

Kamine snapped her head up to him. She didn't realize how distracted she had become.

"How did you even know I had stopped?" she asked.

"Because," he started, leaning back against the wall. He was practically laying down at this point, with his long legs outstretched all the way, and his pants riding up to reveal boring, black socks. His shoulder-length hair was down today, and she could see he had trimmed his beard, a light stubble shadowing his face—not that she was paying him that much attention. "You either move your hands, your head, whisper to yourself, or stare so hard at the rock that your eyes tear up from not blinking for so long."

She supposed that was true, but she hated how easily he could read her.

"I just needed a break."

"You haven't even done anything," he pointed out.

Did he really need to remind her how utterly useless she was? Maybe she should just leave, and tell him she was done with these private lessons. He clearly had no actual interest in teaching her.

"Well..." she began, her whole demeanor deflated. She didn't have a fight within her. What would be the point? It wouldn't change anything. She would still be the same powerless woman. Angering him wouldn't help. "I just don't know what to do."

It hurt to say the words out loud, to admit that no matter how many books she read or how many attempts she made, she had no idea what to do to fix this.

For so long, she had considered that maybe there were no powers brimming beneath her skin. That she was utterly empty of the magic of the court. It was rare, but not impossible. But one day, she had felt the spark of it. It was barely there, just enough to notice. Her mother was having a day of clarity. They both were out in the woods picking berries when a bird flew down and snatched the red fruit from Kamine's fingers. Right as Kamine and her mother laughed, the faintest shudder rocked through Kamine. Kamine recognized it for what it was immediately.

"Lift the rock," he said simply.

"Clearly, I can't," she replied, deadpan. She had no idea why he thought commanding her around would be the solution.

"Try again."

She closed her eyes, wanting to be in her bed instead. Away from him, away from facing her incompetence.

"Try again," he said, more forcefully this time.

She grit her teeth. "What's the point? You aren't even helping."

"Try again," he demanded.

"Why do you even care?"

"Fucking try again!" he yelled. The sound reverberated, and it startled her, how much his own voice was tinged with pain, almost like he was begging. He heaved, his chest rising and falling deeply, as if it took him great effort.

Fine then. She rolled her shoulders and neck. Outstretching her arms, she thought about the rock landing into her palm. She flicked her finger up, and up, and up. She felt nothing. Tears threatened to spill from her eyes, because she was so tired of failing.

Footsteps inched closer, and closer. She ignored how she could practically feel his presence, feel exactly where he stood in relation to her.

From behind her, he touched her shoulders, and dragged his hands to her elbows. His chest was on her back and his breath hot on her neck.

"Relax," he said, soothingly. He brought her arms down, and she willingly let him maneuver her body.

He tugged on her wild, curly hair. Her neck craned backwards.

"Allow yourself to breathe," he said, against her neck. Goose-bumps freckled her skin.

Kamine released a deep breath. She had no idea what was happening, but she could already tell this wouldn't work. Relaxing and breathing were horrible advice. She was trying to move a fucking rock, not sleep.

"Stop fucking thinking," he demanded. His grip was tight on her waist, holding her still as she tried to pull away.

"I don't understand how any of this is helpful."

"You don't have to understand. Just do as I say."

"It's not working."

"Because you're thinking."

"That's what a person with a brain does, they think."

He sighed deeply, and let her go. She turned to him, and they were so close she could see his black eyes and the white veins scattered through them, like they were made of marble. "You need to trust me for this to work."

Her mouth gaped open, but she shut it closed so hard that her teeth clanged together. "Trust? You assaulted me on my first day of class, how could I trust you?"

"Back to that excuse again?"

She pushed him, and he stumbled. His eyes became wide and hard, but after a moment, he brushed it off.

"I deserved that."

"You deserve much worse," she said.

He smiled devilishly, like he was proud of himself. "Glad to see your fight is back."

Kamine didn't know what he meant by that, but the way he held himself made it seem like he was goading her into her anger, that he had purposefully wound her up.

"Are we done?" she asked.

He threw a rock at her, and she didn't have a chance to catch it before it hit her.

"Ouch," Kamine rubbed her thigh.

"Worth a shot."

"You're a horrible teacher."

"You're a horrible student."

She didn't need to listen to him insulting her. She stormed away, but he grabbed her wrist.

"Meet me here tomorrow night."

I'd rather die, Kamine thought, but gave him the response he was looking for. "Fine."

A clap sounded from the entrance of the classroom.

"Such a gracious teacher," Kestra said in a condescending tone. "I remember when you were just like that. Causing trouble, and refusing to back down."

"What do you want, Kestra?" Grimot asked from his spot. The large room seemed to shrink with her presence. He had nowhere to hide or run off to either, since there was only one way out, and one way in.

Kestra smiled as she realized this. She stood in front of the door, daring him to try to leave.

Grimot picked up the book he had abandoned, holding it tight like a security blanket. Then, he weakened his grip, embarrassed that he needed protection from her.

"Is she why you refuse me?"

Grimot couldn't stop the deep and breathy laugh that escaped him, so low in his gut that it could be mistaken for a growl. Kestra always had to find ways to make it about her. When Grimot first arrived at the school, he quickly learned that the monster rumored to prowl the tunnels was her. She sucked the blood from the students and kept returning for more, hungry and determined. For some reason, when her teeth sunk into him, she had difficulty letting go.

"Are you lost?" he asked, not entertaining her unfounded jealousy.

"She's pretty," she said, drawing closer to him now. Her short dress displayed her pale legs, ones that once wrapped around him while he sunk into her. "If you like someone who looks like a lost puppy, that is."

"If you don't actually need me for anything, then you can leave." He tapped the book against his thigh, becoming more agitated with every passing second. He didn't want to escalate anything, but if she touched him, then he would not hesitate to push her away.

"You're so tense."

"I'm tired," he corrected.

She didn't stop approaching him. He stepped backwards. It wasn't that he was scared of *her*. It was that he didn't know if he would want to stop if they started, and *that* truth scared him. He hadn't been with anyone since her. For five years, it had been just his hands.

"I know how to wake you up," she said, her lips popping on the last consonant. She caged him against the wall, her strong floral scent assaulting his senses.

"No."

She stopped, almost as if that one word blew away the cloud of lust from her mind.

"Oh, good," Headmaster Dritoria said, her coily hair framing her sharp face. "I was looking for you both."

Kestra cleared her throat and backed away. Grimot sighed deeply, like breathing for the first time after drowning. Images of Kamine in that deep pool of water flashed before him, how lifeless her body was. He shook them away, recentering himself to the present.

"I wanted to speak about the logistics of the Heart. Grimot currently has it in his room for safekeeping, but Kestra, you'll need to pray to the Weather Gods to tell you where to place it this year." The Heart resided in his room because as a new professor, it was considered an initiation ritual to ensure he took on the role for the right reasons: the wellbeing of the Thunder Court. He stared at the amethyst gem regularly, each time being transported back to the moment he had touched it during his Undertaking.

Kestra and the Headmaster chatted, while Grimot did his best to seem engaged. Conversations about the Heart always made him uncomfortable. Everytime he walked into his room, he wanted to shatter it, but he now had a responsibility for its safekeeping. He would be damned if he let his emotions get in the way of accomplishing what he had set out to do.

Nine

"Let's go," Professor Grimot said as soon as Kamine entered the classroom for their next session.

"So demanding," she whispered under her breath. His hands clenched at her words, but she wouldn't apologize.

He led her out of the room, and charged through the halls, even with a slight limp Kamine hadn't noticed before. Perhaps he hurt himself. Kamine was nearly running just to keep up with him, but she refused to lose him through this maze of a school. Even though it had been a few weeks in, she still struggled to navigate the place. She could have sworn the halls moved at night to trick everyone. Janina thought that was the most ridiculous thing ever. She said mountains don't move that way. Maybe not all mountains, but this one...Kamine wouldn't be surprised to learn if the walls of this place were crafted by the hands of Goddess Buraza, herself.

"I thought we were having another lesson," Kamine hissed as she almost twisted her ankle on the uneven ground.

"Don't ask questions, just follow," he responded.

He always had to boss her around, didn't he? Kamine kept quiet, more for her sake than his. She had no idea where they were headed, but she could feel the slight decline of their path.

Since Kamine was taking private lessons, she no longer had to attend actual class. At least not for now, Professor Grimot told her. Headmaster Dritoria had apparently been informed of these lessons, and she had agreed that Kamine should not overexert herself.

Janina and Zoya filled her in on how things were progressing with everyone in class. They were continuing one-on-one practice. Apparently, Professor Grimot had them throw one rock between the two of them, and they had to work together to keep it afloat. The professor would then ring a bell, and they competed to see who could shoot the rock at the other person first. It tested their diligence and speed. It sounded like Kamine's nightmare, but her friends both enjoyed the exercises, and thought they were helping.

Kamine spent her extra time reading one of the few books she brought from home. She would need to find a library soon, because she was nearing the end of her stash. A problem for another day.

They ventured down some stairs, and Kamine could feel the air growing thicker. She swore she heard a trickle of water somewhere too. For the first time in weeks, she felt that connection with the earth that she had been missing, her body closer to the ground, perhaps even within the depths of it, with the soil and dirt a short distance away.

Instead of losing focus, she memorized the path as best as she could, so she could find her way back. Knowing the professor, he would leave her to fend for herself after whatever hell he was about to put her through.

Professor Grimot abruptly stopped and turned towards her. Kamine startled and almost fell backwards, but he steadied her. He held onto her shoulders for a moment longer than necessary, and when he pulled away, he looked at his palms, as if she had burned him.

He cleared his throat.

"When we get in there," he started, his tone serious, "don't think too much. Allow yourself to be present in the moment."

Kamine narrowed her eyes. That was the closest thing to good advice he had ever given her. She didn't know what it meant exactly, but her heart skipped a beat at the anxiety of facing the unknown. Her palms began to sweat, too. She hated being surprised.

"And," he added, right before they entered, "don't use your hands."

Grimot had no idea if forcing Kamine to come to this would be good for her, but sometimes, an unexpected shove was exactly what someone needed. Not something deadly, like her attempt with the baths, but something challenging. He just hoped she wouldn't get herself killed. He promised himself to keep a close eye on her, and use his own powers if it called for it. He didn't need Headmaster Dritoria up his ass for getting one of her students hurt again.

Kamine stopped as soon as she entered. Her eyes were wide, unsure, but they hardened when she saw that the rest of the cohort was here, too. Along with some new faces: past Undertaking participants.

It was tradition, one he explained to the current cohort during class. Kamine wasn't there to hear it, and he questioned if he wanted to let her know. She hadn't improved. At all. But...there was some kind of spark in her that made him tell her to come. He had a feeling she would have hated being left out.

"What is this?" she whispered.

"A game."

She gulped, and he could see the flutter of her pulse in her neck. She was nervous. He would be too if he was in her position. This game was brutal, and it required skill she didn't have.

Janina and Zoya waved at Kamine, but the rest of the cohort seemed to slow their warm-ups. They must be wondering why the fuck someone like her would be allowed to do this.

She faced him. "So what's the goal?"

At least she was still eager to learn, though her body was tense. That wouldn't work in this game. One had to be limber and quick.

She fidgeted with something on her wrist under the sleeve of her training clothes, and a gleam of gold peaked out for a moment. His hands itched to soothe her, to drag his fingers across her skin until she relaxed into his touch. He stiffened at his own thoughts, though, brushing them away.

"There are two teams, one on each side of the line." He pointed to it, and her eyes trailed the long white line across the room. "Other than that, it's simple. Each team throws rocks at each other and you dodge them, either using your own powers or with quick reflexes. If you get hit, you're out. Whichever team is left standing, wins."

"That sounds deadly."

"That's why we'll all be wearing metal armor. It's a way for you to get comfortable moving in it."

Kamine shook her head. "I'm not ready for something like this. Look at them. They have a hunger for death in their eyes."

He came up to her and guided her jaw up with his finger, giving into his desire to touch her skin and meet her gaze. "Exactly why it's perfect. You won't have time to think. Let your body do what it is meant to do."

Grimot didn't allow her to object anymore. He whistled and the whole room had their eyes on him now, but his remained on Kamine's violet eyes, brimming with anticipation. "Get your gear on, and we'll begin."

Kamine fell in line beside her friends, who both appeared skeptical of the situation, like they couldn't actually believe that Kamine was about to be subjected to this. She just shrugged, attempting to be as nonchalant about this as possible.

Unfortunately, that false easiness wavered as soon as the teams were announced. It was the current cohort against the past Undertaking participants. One of those participants was a former winner, too.

Kamine was so nervous that she prayed to whatever Weather Gods were listening that she made it out alive, and mostly unscathed.

Janina tightened the metal plates on her arms. "Just stay behind us."

Zoya nodded. "We'll protect you."

A sweet sentiment, but Kamine knew that if she stayed back for too long, she might end up as the last one standing on their team. Then she would be truly fucked.

"Thanks, but I think my strategy will be to dodge as many rocks as possible, and then purposefully get hit."

Kamine told herself that she at least had to look like she was trying for as long as possible. Otherwise, she had a feeling that Professor Grimot would give her hell during their next lesson. Kamine was quick, at least. She had that going for herself. She also had the advantage that the other team didn't know her weakness yet, so she just had to pretend that she knew what she was doing.

Kamine clasped the helmet on her head. Wearing armor was foreign to her. It was heavy and made it harder to move. But Kamine would be grateful for it during the Undertaking as large boulders pelted the ground around her.

Her cohort and the competing team got into position. Kamine chose somewhere towards the right, and closer to the back than the front. She needed some time to gauge how the opposing team would play. Maybe her team would be lucky, and they'd take it easy. Kamine doubted it, especially as she finally took a long look at them. These former participants were eager to wreck shit up.

Professor Grimot blew a whistle, and the game began. All the rocks sitting on the line rose up and moved. It was hard to tell who was moving which rock with their powers, so she just focused on anything coming at her.

A rock blasted by, almost hitting Roz, but the pink-haired woman gritted her teeth as she stopped the rock's trajectory with her powers, tossing it back to the other side. She moved with such grace and such little fear. She belonged in this type of setting, where she could let free all the rage that boiled inside her.

Kamine got so distracted by watching her that she almost got hit. She dove down to her knees at the last moment, and felt her whole body protest at the sudden movement. Sweat began to coat her brow as the intensity of the game ramped up around her.

It took her a moment with the restrictive armor, but once she got back up, the scene before her had her heart racing up her throat. Half of her team was out on the sidelines already, while the other team still stood strong.

She snuck a quick glance at Professor Grimot, but his attention was on the rest of the game, calling people out once they were hit.

A rock swooshed by her, realizing a team member on the opposing side had found their next target. His yellow eyes were determined to get her. Kamine shook her hands, a habit she had developed when she tried using her powers.

"Don't use your hands!" She heard Professor Grimot yell, but she couldn't spare him a glance.

Another rock blasted at her, and she slid to the right, while another one was already on its way. She fell to her stomach to avoid it, her palms flat on the floor beneath her.

It brought her back, back to the time she hid under her bed in this exact position. On her stomach, scared and alone, until her mother showed up, and had reached out a hand to her. Kamine didn't understand why the world was falling then, but she had understood her mother's offer of safety.

Kamine's blink bridged her back to the present. The room was yelling. She didn't know if it was at her, or just the overall energy in the room. Either way, she stayed down, thinking about her comfort place, the forest that welcomed her. She thought of her bare feet digging into the dirt, allowing it to coat her skin in a protective layer.

A harsh pound dropped on the back of her left calf, and she yelped at the shooting pain. A spasm traveled across her whole leg, up to her thigh, and then to her bare hands on the ground. Her fingers pressed down just like they would press against mud to leave an indentation of her hand.

Then, the world beneath her hand sprung down, her body melting into the floor before it moved back up, like a gentle wave of water.

"Kamine! Out!" She barely heard it through all the noise, but she couldn't get up. Out of embarrassment or shock, Kamine's body *refused* to get up. It was like the ground didn't want to let her go.

She gritted her teeth as she strained with her weak arms to lift her upper body, but her arms were shaking with the effort. Kamine could bet all eyes were on her, and once she got into a sitting position, she was not surprised that the whole room was staring.

"I need a moment," she breathed out.

She expected Professor Grimot to drag her to her feet, but instead he walked over, crouched down to her level, pulled the helmet off her head, and hissed, "What the fuck?"

She closed her eyes, and drooped her head down. Her unruly hair draped over her face. *Good*, she didn't need everyone to see how red her face burned.

"I just need to rest a moment," she repeated in a whisper, barely able to get the words out between the deep intakes of breath. She would get up soon, she just needed a break. The world around her had changed and she just needed to orient herself again.

"You're drained," he said, in a sense of disbelief. She didn't understand why. She had just gotten hit so hard that she expected her leg to be broken.

"I think I'll need help getting up."

Professor Grimot stripped off her arm and chest plates, and it was such a relief to be able to move her body freely, without the constriction of metal.

"You'll need more than that."

That was the last thing she heard before her eyes fell shut and her body went limp into Grimot's arms.

Ten

Grimot carried Kamine's motionless body through Skola's halls. He had checked for a pulse, and it thrummed beneath her light skin—weak, but there.

The incline of the ground made his journey just that much harder, but he barely felt the burn of his calves, barely felt anything but his absolute fear for her well-being.

"You're gonna get me in trouble again," he grumbled to no one but himself. He told the others that the game was over right before he left, and everyone had dispersed.

"Is she dead?" Zoya whispered, the woman's voice shaky as she tried to keep up with his pace.

"Be careful," Janina warned, when he almost bumped Kamine into the wall as he made a sharp turn.

He could feel the body in his arms begin to shift, as if trying to go to the sound of her friend's voices. He tightened his hold on her, not letting her fall.

"She needs space, not to be hounded," he said. Listening to him, both of Kamine's friends backed off, allowing him to take control of the situation.

He stopped at the first lounge area he could find, and rested her on the plush couch.

"Stay here," he said, as if she could even hear him in her state.

He rushed to find some water and a rag. When he returned, she was still laying there, unmoving. He should tell Dritoria about this, but he couldn't just leave her. Kamine would be confused and scared if she woke up alone.

He placed the wet rag on her forehead and sat on a couch opposite her. The faint spell would wear off soon. He was all too familiar with using too much power at once, but overtime, her well of power would return, along with a pounding headache, and a ravenous hunger.

The shift under their feet had shocked everyone, and had thrown them all off balance. At first, nobody knew where the quake had come from. Perhaps the court was being attacked, or the mountain was just settling. Then everyone's attention gravitated to Kamine's body on the ground, crouched and shaking. Nobody could believe it—*he* couldn't believe it—until he saw her ashen face, her purple eyes usually so bright, now dimmed.

That's when he ran to her. While he didn't know when his indifference towards her turned to care, he didn't dare question it now.

There was a powerful gift hiding under her skin. It just wasn't what anyone expected. It was unlike anything he'd ever witnessed before.

It was dangerous if she didn't learn how to control it. If she used her powers improperly during the Undertaking, she could damn the whole court. If she was as powerful as Grimot now presumed, then she could rearrange the very ground they walked on.

Kamine gasped awake and practically rolled off the couch. Her eyes blinked rapidly, adjusting to the light, and landing directly on him.

"Where am I?" she asked.

"Do you remember anything?"

She narrowed her eyes and shifted into a seated position, clenching and unclenching her hands. She looked so frail now. How could that petite body cause something potentially catastrophic?

Her voice cracked, as she clutched her wrist to ensure the bracelet was still there. When she confirmed it was, she answered. "No. I mean I was at that game, on the ground, and then everything went black."

So she didn't remember what she had done. That wasn't surprising. Anyone using their powers for the first time could wipe themselves out if they weren't careful. The fact that she was older and her body wasn't accustomed to it meant that the effects must have been more intense.

"We have a lot of work to do," he said.

"What do you mean?"

"You have powers, Kamine. Powers that could kill us all."

Kamine must have fallen asleep. When she woke up, her whole body ached. She adjusted herself to get more comfortable, and as she moved onto her side, she almost slipped out of the couch.

"It's a mystery how someone like you received the powers you did," Professor Grimot said from his own position on the opposite couch. He flipped a page in his book.

A soft blanket was wrapped around her legs, a feeling of warmth and safety.

"I think I need a recap of everything that transpired," Kamine responded. Someone had taken her shoes off and brushed out her tight braid from earlier.

Everything from the last few hours—at least she thought it was only hours—had become foggy in her mind, like a window covered in condensation.

"There's not much to say," he said. "You had powers all along. It just took that game to finally get them to come out, or more likely your mind finally figured out exactly what was needed to call them out."

Kamine wondered why that was. It wasn't the first time she found herself in a life-threatening situation, and yet, her powers had never shown themselves, then. So what was different this time? Maybe it was as simple as the fact she was thinking too much about using her powers in all her previous attempts.

"I think it was because you were close to the ground."

Kamine whipped her head to him, but he was still reading his book. "What?"

He shut the book. The fireplace crackled with flames, giving a warm glow to his face. It outlined his strong nose and sharp chin. His hair was pulled back tightly into a bun.

"Your whole body was on the ground when everything shook, your hands directly on it. You've tried so many pointless techniques, but likely never tried laying on the ground."

Kamine supposed not. It wouldn't make sense to do that if she were trying to get a rock to float. With these powers, on the other hand, it seemed reasonable that getting down to ground level would help her connect with her magic.

"I guess I should thank you, then?" she asked.

His fingers stopped their gentle tapping on the leather cover of the book. "Now, we need to train this power so that you can do it standing. Relying on having to lie down during your Undertaking would be a death sentence."

"I'm not even sure how this power will help. Moving the ground doesn't stop the falling rocks from hitting anything. I'd likely just kill someone by causing homes to crumble on top of innocent lives."

"So we hone it," he said seriously. He turned his palms upward and a few rocks pulled towards his palms, like he had a magnet in his bones. "All of our powers can destroy. It's one of the first things we learn to do with it. The next step is putting everything back together. That part is harder to master, some never do."

"And you're willing to take on that role for me? To *actually* teach me?" *Instead of just sitting by,* she thought, but didn't voice.

He faced her fully now, and rested his elbows on his thighs. His white sleeves were rolled up, revealing his muscular arms, with those two stones in his clavicle on full display. "I'm your magic professor, am I not? I would be failing at my job if I didn't."

He said it with arrogance, but there was something deeper in those black eyes, as if he was making a promise with himself that failure was not an option. For some reason, Kamine was now a part of that internalized decree, and she couldn't afford to fail him. They were in too deep. She just wondered what methods he would employ to get her powers to unleash, and then tame.

❖

Eleven

"I heard Kamine had some kind of breakthrough," Dritoria said. Though her tone shifted to displeasure as she added, "After I heard that she almost got killed again."

Professor Grimot and Headmaster Dritoria were in the first room of the school—the only room where any sun filtered through. With a metal watering pot in hand, she nurtured the few plants that basked in the light of the school's one rare window. She looked so at peace as the sun lit her face, her dark skin glowing. *She belonged out in the world,* he thought. Not in this dark hellhole. But she was dedicated to her students, and he applauded her for the sacrifice.

Grimot had been on his way to his room and, unfortunately, had bumped into the Headmaster. He knew he would need to explain himself. Word spread that Kamine had been hurt, *again*. It wasn't directly his fault this time, but he was still to blame for even bringing her to the game, despite it being a tradition that Headmaster Dritoria sanctioned and surely participated in, herself, years ago.

"Correct," he finally responded, hands clasped behind his back. "Her powers are much greater than any of us could have expected. I'm now working to ensure that she can use them properly."

Dritoria stepped on a small ladder to reach a few plants that hung from random perches of rock. "Good, she needs to learn to control it."

"I'll do my best," he said, relieved that he didn't get any stern words thrown at him for allowing Kamine to get into such a precarious situation in the first place. Maybe Headmaster Dritoria was also relieved that progress had been made with Kamine's powers.

Grimot helped the Headmaster down from the step ladder. Her face became solemn, weary. "I worry for her, Grimot."

He cocked his head to the right. "What for?"

He could guess what for. He had treated her harshly from the start, and Headmaster Dritoria no longer trusted him to teach her in a safe manner.

"Her mother became a ghost after her Undertaking."

Well, that was not where he thought it was going...

She continued, "She was such a light when she entered this school with me."

"You were in the same cohort?"

She dipped her chin. "Kassandra was so confident in herself, and it showed in her powers. She could move boulders across the entire room on her first day. She had such strength, and so much love."

Grimot gulped, not liking where this was heading.

"No one knows the full extent of what she experienced during the Undertaking since no one witnessed it. Kamine's father, Jace, hasn't spoken on it either. The following years after her Undertaking seemed good, at least from the outside. She married Jace right after she won, then had Kamine and Damien. Yet none of it brightened the shadow that loomed over her. She could no longer find the sun, and her life ended too soon."

"Undertakings change a person," he said, wanting to offer something, *anything*. He knew the exact feeling, though. One's life was lived in anticipation of being an Undertaking participant. If chosen, it was an honor, but a large responsibility, with each death in the village weighing on the shoulders of the cohort that failed to prevent it.

"Yes," the Headmaster agreed. "They do, which is why I put so much effort into hammering in the importance of understanding what it means to be a participant. It's more than just finding the Heart."

Grimot understood that. He hadn't when he was an actual participant, but it was clearer for him only now that it was too late, when his body would be frozen to stone if he didn't accomplish what the Gods set out for him to do.

The Headmaster put a hand on his shoulder. "Kamine never got to experience the version of her mother that was full of life. She has only seen how an Undertaking can strip a person down to a husk. Be patient with her as you embark on this journey. It's more than just her powers. There's an emotional wall holding her back. One I hope you can help her crack away at."

"You're alive," Zoya cheered as Kamine limped into the Purple Hall. She dove off her bed and gave Kamine a hug. Kamine winced, but returned it as best as she could.

Janina gave her two thumbs up. "That was quite a show back there."

Kamine rubbed her head, "Was it? I barely remember it."

Zoya gently guided her to the bottom bunk. Kamine immediately dropped to her back so she could stare at the bottom of the top bunk. Writing covered it. Everything from profanities, to simple drawings. In one corner, there was a heart with two initials in it.

"Professor Grimot looked so worried," Zoya said, as she pulled Kamine's boots off her feet. It felt good to stretch her toes.

"He was probably just trying to cover his ass."

"No, he looked genuinely worried," Janina jumped in. "He lifted you up, and practically ran you out the room like a white knight."

They must have been imagining it. Professor Grimot worried about her? That sounded like some romantic fantasy they concocted to make her feel less embarrassed about the whole thing. The reality was that Professor Grimot was doing everything in his power to make her miserable.

Kamine pushed herself up off the mattress to be able to see her friends. Zoya had knitting needles and the beginning of a blanket that she promised Kamine would be done by the time of the Undertaking. Janina was holding the ball of yarn for her, but her face revealed no hint of deceit. They honestly believed Professor Grimot cared.

Nothing between them had actually changed since he started his private lessons with her. He was still a menace, but perhaps he did show—in the small moments—that he actually had a caring bone in his body. He had given her advice, even if it hadn't seemed the most helpful.

And then...he had watched over her as she rested. He hadn't left her side, and he had even walked her almost all the way to her room, only leaving her right at the mouth of the hallway that led to her room where her friends had waited. His parting words were the quiet advice that she needed to find something to eat. Kamine hadn't even realized how ravenous she had become until he pointed it out. Over the last few days, she had discovered he made her comfortable.

Kamine didn't know what to make of it all. But she was convinced his actions were definitely for his own personal gain, somehow. She was sure of it.

Yet, there was a tiny whisper in the back of her head that kept telling her there was something more, that him using his spare time to teach her was bigger than the satisfaction of training the untrainable student. But...what?

Twelve

Kamine rubbed her arms. She still felt sore from the game even though two days had passed. She rested each moment she could, spent long hours reading in bed, which meant she had no books left. She promised herself that tonight after dinner she would go searching for a library.

First, she needed to get through this lesson. For the first time in ever, there was a buzzing energy to her steps. A newfound exhilaration because she had the confirmation she needed: her powers existed. Somewhere within her bones and veins flowed the power that she longed for her whole life. Now, it was only a matter of harnessing it.

Professor Grimot also seemed more enthusiastic. He was actually standing with her, and not distracting himself with a book, completely ignoring her presence. It was a step in the right direction.

"I don't want you to learn to use laying down as a crutch," he started. "But I want you to be reminded of what it felt like to get your powers out, so this will be the one and only time I will allow you to do it."

Kamine nodded. She awkwardly sat on the ground. Laying on her stomach felt too vulnerable in this environment because her face would be pressing downwards, and it would be harder to get back up. She chose to lay on her back, giving her the ability to see the Professor easily at all times.

She pressed her palms on the hard stone. The grittiness bit into her skin, and it energized her, like the rocks were fueling her up.

"Remember, it's not about fear, it's not about imagining it. It's an extension of you, just like walking and breathing. When you think too hard about doing those basic things, you stumble."

He backed away from her, giving her space. Kamine closed her eyes. Instead of thinking about her powers, she thought of her family, of the day Damien was born. Kamine had been eighteen, her mother's pregnancy unexpected. Not that her parents hadn't tried for another child, but many attempts didn't stick.

Both Kamine and her father hoped that new life would bring light back to her mother. For a short time, it did. Her mother cried with tears of joy when Damien was put into her arms. Those early days were some of the happiest days of Kamine's life.

Damien completed their family. He filled a hole that no one even knew existed. He was a happy baby who smiled at everyone and barely fussed. It was almost impossible to separate her mother from the babe. She held him constantly; her ear at his chest, listening to his heartbeats.

But something changed, one day when her mother was bathing him in the kitchen sink. Kamine heard Damien's cries from her room, and rushed into the kitchen, since it was so out of the ordinary for him.

The scene she found scarred her. Her mother was nowhere to be found, while Damian lay in the sink with water pouring over his face. He couldn't breathe. Kamine pulled his slippery body out of the water, and held him close. Kamine looked out the window, and noticed her mother was outside, standing, staring out into the fields. Another Undertaking was soon approaching.

"Stop using your hands," Professor Grimot reprimanded.

Kamine's eyes flew open. She didn't realize she had her arms outstretched, as if she were reaching for her little brother, or for her mother who was already lost. It was days later, right before that year's Undertaking, that she had taken her life.

Kamine lowered her arms again, letting go of the direction of her morbid thoughts. "Did anything happen?"

She didn't feel the ground bend, but she also had been so lost in the memory.

"No," he said with a huff. He came towards her with something in his hands.

"What are you doing?" she said, becoming nervous as he took her hands.

"Do you trust that I am doing everything in your best interest?"

"What?"

"Answer. Yes or no."

Kamine didn't understand, but those dark black eyes convinced her to agree.

"Yes."

He grabbed her hands and bound her wrists together with a sturdy piece of rope, leaving her at his mercy.

Grimot tightened the knot enough to prevent escape, but not too much that Kamine would begin to panic. He could already see the anxiety brewing in her eyes.

He kneeled at her feet, watching her chest rise and fall, her training clothes conforming perfectly to her body. Her gasps grew more frantic. She needed to relax for this to work. Either nothing would happen in her current state, or she would cause mass destruction.

"Relax," he said, placing his hands on her shins.

She tensed at his touch at first, but then her legs loosened slightly under him. Her breathing still hadn't evened out, though. He smoothed his hands higher, to her thighs.

She snapped her attention to him. "What are you doing?"

"Massaging your thighs." He pressed his knuckles into them and made small circles.

"And why, may I ask?" she bit out through gritted teeth.

"You're too tense. I don't want the school to be destroyed. You can't lose control."

His fingers dug into her plush thighs as he continued. She moaned, and her face turned red. "Sorry."

He didn't say anything, instead focusing on his ministrations of her legs, going up and down. But his cock stirred. It wanted to hear that sound again. *He* wanted to hear it, while he was deep inside her, ideally.

He wondered with the way she arched her back just now, if she wanted it, too.

Clearing his throat, he dismissed such thoughts. "Do you feel your powers?"

She shook her head. Her eyes were clamped shut.

"Do you feel anything like you did during the game?"

"No," she managed to get out. "Nothing."

"How did you feel? What was going through your head?"

Kamine lay there, as if thinking hard.

"I was resigned to whatever fate awaited me. I was ready to accept any outcome."

Grimot stopped his work on her legs. This was going to happen, then. Sex could be a catalyst for one's power. His first time with someone, he climaxed so hard he cracked a nearby boulder. It wasn't the safest method, but if it could help her...

"What?" she asked as she lifted her neck up. "Did something happen?" Her lips were swollen from biting them as she concentrated, her curly hair fanned out.

"Do you trust me?"

Grimot tracked the bob of her throat.

"Not really."

Grimot quirked his lips. He crawled up her body, hovering just over her.

He flattened his hand just above her core. "I need a yes." He said, sternly. He wouldn't take that step if she didn't want it.

Kamine's eyes focused on his hand that trembled where she wanted him, then flicked to meet his gaze.

"Yes," she breathed out.

Grimot groaned as soon as he placed his hand on her swollen cunt. The fabric was damp, and he loved knowing it was because of him.

Kamine had lost control. Her body and mind warred with themselves, one craving his touch, the other demanding her to push him away.

"Lay back," he whispered into her ear, and the way his voice growled, all trains of thought were wiped away. "Accept that this is happening."

So she did. Kamine rested back on the ground, her hands still tied above her head.

Grimot gently rubbed at first, circling the swollen nub over her clothes. She hissed at the sensation, how easily he wound her up.

"Do you like that?" he asked as she rocked up into his hands. He smiled. "Or do you like it harder?" He pressed his fingers down, and she moaned loudly in response. "Good to know."

He continued, changing the patterns he made, the tempo—and with each brush of his fingers, Kamine relented every part of herself to this moment. She didn't care about anything else except for how he worked to wring out the orgasm that began to surface.

"Don't stop," she whimpered, tears forming in her eyes. "I'm so close."

He immediately took his hands off her.

She gasped. "I said, don't!"

"Stop thinking," he gritted out. "I'm in control."

She narrowed her eyes angrily, but leaned back again and closed them.

"Get on your knees," he ordered.

"I'm a little tied up at the moment," she shot back, growing frustrated at the loss of his touch.

"Don't be a brat, Kamine."

She stared at him, but she yielded to his command. He sat back and watched as she awkwardly got on her knees, and placed her tied hands on the ground.

He pulled her pants and panties down to reveal her lush backside. She knew she was slick with heat, and for a moment, thoughts of him driving his cock right into her without warning flashed before her. He went slow, though, as he dragged his fingers through her folds. She shivered as he sucked on them, and moaned.

"You taste better than the finest wine," he said against her backside.

He flicked her clit. She breathed out, her eyes still shut, and then, he plunged his fingers into her core, using his other hand to knead on her clit.

Right before she climaxed, the ground beneath them shuddered. They swayed, but he didn't stop at the interruption, instead driving deeper until he reached the innermost part. When she tightened around his fingers, she screamed.

Professor Grimot eased her slowly out of it.

She laid down onto her stomach and turned around. Her eyes fluttered open. Her cheeks were stained with the faintest blush.

Then the reality of everything that transpired hit her, what they had done. She let her Professor fuck her, and instead of feeling shame and guilt, she wanted more of him. *All* of him.

He backed away when he noticed that shift in her, and started untying the knots. Once her arms were freed, she pulled her pants back up.

She opened her mouth to speak, but immediately snapped it shut. Instead of trying to make sense of these strange new feelings, she scrambled to her feet and bolted from the room.

Thirteen

Kamine's wrists were red and sore. She pulled down her sleeves as she stormed through the halls in an effort to cover the aggressive marks, in case she passed anyone. Kamine knew she wouldn't be able to stomach dinner. Not now.

Wanting privacy to think, she headed straight for her room while trying her best to avoid anyone who might be lingering in the halls. She didn't want to come face-to-face with any cohorts, because she had a feeling they would be able to read what had transpired on her face. The whole school would know before she even had a moment to herself, to process what had happened.

Kamine shuddered at the thought, pushing forward.

It's not that she regretted it—she had wanted it. *Badly.* But now she wouldn't be able to look into Professor Grimot's dark eyes without thinking of what his fingers were capable of.

"Kamine, is it?"

Kamine jumped at the voice that came from the offshoot of a hall to her right. Clicking footsteps approached her, then the figure was illuminated clearly by a low-hanging sconce.

"Yes…" she said, unsure of exactly who she was speaking to.

She had never seen this woman before. She was tall, with long, golden brown hair that hung down in smooth waves. Her black dress barely reached her mid-thigh. It was the cold determination in her eyes that truly made Kamine hesitate.

The woman smiled. "Headmaster Dritoria has spoken so highly of your mother. I couldn't wait to have a chance to meet you." She assessed Kamine from her feet, up. "Look at you. You're a darling."

"Who are you?" Kamine asked.

"I'm Kestra. Assistant to Headmaster Dritoria."

Oh, Kamine thought. She didn't realize that role existed. To be fair, besides that first day and when Grimot publicly apologized to her, Kamine had barely seen the Headmaster at all. The professors seemed to run the place. It made sense, Kamine supposed, that Headmaster Dritoria needed help with her copious duties.

"I'm also the minister to the Weather Gods," Kestra added as she cocked her head to the right.

"Nice to meet you," Kamine said with a rush. "I should go."

"Not so fast," Kestra said. "I heard you are getting private lessons from Grim."

Grim? She hadn't heard anyone use that nickname for Professor Grimot, and she didn't like the sound of it, if she was being honest.

Kamine nodded. "We're slowly making headway with my powers." And she was slowly becoming infatuated with him, too.

"He has always been so great in one-on-one situations. He's such a master with his gifts." Kestra said, as if she held a deep secret.

Kamine didn't understand Kestra's implication, but she agreed only to end the conversation quickly. Kamine didn't want to spend another second here with this woman. She needed to lie down and sleep off the last hour. Actually, she would take a long bath first, to rinse away his phantom touch.

"I'm grateful that he's taking the time to help me."

Kestra grabbed Kamine's chin. "Let's hope that all that hard work pays off in the Undertaking."

Even sleep wouldn't grace her with oblivion. A part of Kamine feared that her subconscious would dream of him, of his hands roaming her body, of his body on top of hers as he rolled his hips into her core.

The bad thing about having a roommate was that she couldn't relieve herself of this lusty fog.

Another part of Kamine couldn't wipe Kestra's words from her mind. They hung in her subconscious like bright, red apples hanging from a tree branch. She wanted to yank them down, but they were too far for her to reach.

So Kamine picked up her shoes and tiptoed out of her bedroom, being careful to not wake Zoya up.

After Janina and Zoya arrived back from dinner, Kamine had barely been able to look at them. She busied herself with writing a letter to her father and brother, instead.

Her friends asked her about her lesson, and if she made any additional progress. She did her best to keep a straight face as she told them she was able to move the ground again. Thankfully, they didn't ask her how she had done it this time. She didn't even have a lie ready. She was fully prepared to spill out the truth.

Once she leveled her emotions, she would tell her friends what had happened. She needed an outlet. For now though, the secret stuck with her.

With the absence of windows, the hallways looked no different during the day than they did at night. It was always so dark that she needed the lit sconces to make her way through. The energy was different now, though. During the day, she expected to run into someone. Now, she didn't, which made the dim tunnels all the more ominous.

She had no idea if a library even existed in this place, but it was a school, so it would be remiss of her to not seek one out.

For some reason, the late night air—or perhaps the lack of fresh air—made her think of her parents. How they both walked these halls, too, when they were her age. How even in this gilded cage they had fallen in love. Her father had said the moment he laid eyes on her mother, he knew he would dedicate every moment showing his love to her. Even in her mother's cathartic state, he held true to that vow.

Kamine was too stressed about the Undertaking to even think of the possibility of pursuing something romantic. At least emotionally. Physically...was apparently a different matter.

"Where are you going?"

Kamine whipped around, her hand on her chest as her heart rate escalated. Her heart calmed when she realized it was just Professor Grimot, but her body tightened underneath her sleeping clothes.

She crossed her arms, taking a hesitant step back. "I'm looking for a library." Gesturing towards the tunnels, she admitted, "I don't even know if there is a library."

"There isn't."

She grumbled. "What school doesn't have a library?"

"At least not one that's public," he amended. He hesitated as he stared behind her, refusing to make eye contact. "I have my own personal stash."

"Is that an invitation, or a way to show off?"

He shrugged. "Both."

She finally took a moment to study him. He looked disheveled and flustered. His hair was in a haphazard bun, his sleeves rolled up, his buttons undone. Was he also affected by what they had done earlier? Did he regret it?

She had strong feelings about it, too, but regret was not one of them. Desire for more was more like it, though she wasn't ready to admit that, if he didn't feel the same.

But this invitation...what did it mean?

"Are you coming?" he asked. His lips pursed into a tight line when he noticed the double meaning.

She pushed up her glasses that had since slipped down her nose. "An opportunity to judge your reading tastes? Of course, I'll go."

He grunted, but led her along. He purposefully kept his distance from her, his long strides making it difficult for her to keep up. The way to his room was confusing, and they didn't pass anything that looked familiar to her. There were so many right turns at one point, she definitely thought that he was toying with her and taking her in circles.

Then, they reached a long hallway. There were no colored lights like the student's halls had. In fact, beside the one light in the far distance Kamine could barely make out, the hall was dark. A shiver sliced through her as almost complete darkness blanketed them.

A hand touched her shoulder, and Kamine squeaked.

"It's just me," Professor Grimot said, flatly.

"Didn't anyone tell you to not sneak up on people."

"I wouldn't call it sneaking when we're the only two in the hall-way, and you know I'm here with you."

"You never know," she shot back. "There could be a ghost here with us."

He scoffed, "I promise there are no ghosts here. I scared them away."

"How comforting."

She was grateful that at least they were still comfortable enough with each other to make light-hearted jabs.

"And what about the monster?" She crossed her arms, curious to see how he would respond.

His face turned serious, his jaw tense. "The monster won't be bothering us."

She expected a mean jibe back at her for believing in such tales, but he only looked sincere. Kamine didn't question him further, even though his reaction told her there was more to that response than he was letting on. They continued their way over, the light still so far away. Perhaps the light was an illusion, perhaps they would move forward forever and never reach it.

"Why do you get such a private room?"

He tightened his hands on her shoulder. "Everyone's room here is relatively private."

"I have to share with a roommate."

He sucked in a breath. "Right. I hated that."

She hummed. "I actually like it. Maybe that's because Zoya knits me blankets to help keep me warm."

"You wouldn't believe that she was so warm if you saw her in a classroom. Her refined skills mean that she can weave a storm of small rocks around a person with such precision that she can land one in someone's mouth, if she tries hard enough."

Kamine blinked, so unused to having such a civil conversation with him, much less one where he was praising anyone. It was re-freshing. It made that fluttering feeling in her stomach grow.

He pushed open the door to his room, and Kamine gasped at the sight before her. The walls were lined with shelves and shelves of books. An endless array of colors and covers. Kamine stepped inside, and trailed her finger down one of the worn spines.

"History?" she asked.

Professor Grimot shrugged. "I like nonfiction."

"Not me," she said, her voice shaking with a storm of excitement. "I have always found comfort in fiction. If my own powers didn't want to work, then at least I could read about fictional characters whose powers did. It almost felt safer than actually trying to get my magic to come out. Less dangerous."

She didn't know why she offered that information to him. Maybe it was because he had brought her here, around his prized possessions, ones that revealed a lot about his soul. That's what books could do. They dug deep into the innermost part of someone, and pulled out pieces of them that they didn't know existed. Showing Kamine his collection was a vulnerable thing, and she didn't take that lightly.

When she turned around, his hands were in his pockets as he stared at her. "What?"

He shook his head. "Nothing."

She wanted to push, but she left it at that. There would be other occasions to hound him for his secrets.

"Do you have a favorite?" she wondered as she gazed at all the titles.

He whistled. "That's the hardest question you can ask someone."

"Fine, is there one you would recommend to someone like me?"

He pondered for a moment, looking up and squinting his eyes as if the Gods themselves would procure an answer for him. The warm glow of the room highlighted his strong features. She saw clearly as his throat bobbed, and Kamine had the desire to lick it.

He went to one of the shelves, and scanned the books before pulling one out, and handing it to her.

"*The Tales of Love and Tragedy*?"

"It's a collection of short stories. They're based on true events. Someone found a collection of letters, and wrote stories based on the exchanges this couple had. The final story, as you would expect, ends tragically."

"I don't think I need more tragedy in my life," Kamine whispered, more to herself than to him.

"I suppose not, but the love story within this makes the tragedy seem not so tragic."

She handed the book back to him. "I think I'll pass for now."

"You miss her, your mother?"

Kamine nodded, blinking away the sting of tears in her eyes. "Even if the mother I knew wasn't the one my father fell in love with, or the one that won her Undertaking, she was still *my* mother. Even if she was changed, that was the only version I knew." Kamine caught glimpses of what her mother was like before while she was pregnant with Damien, but there was never any strong affection towards Kamine. Just a gentle calmness that Kamine hadn't witnessed before.

Grimot bit his lip, as if fighting an internal battle. "Come with me."

Kamine followed him into another room. His bedroom. The bed was made, the wool covers tucked in perfectly, and the pillows fluffed. He kept such order.

He cleared his throat. "This way."

Kamine's face heated, but he just gestured to the bust of Buraza on his dresser. In one of the eyes was an amethyst gem.

"Is—" She swallowed. "Is that the Heart?"

The purple glow of the gemstone practically called to Kamine, as if it recognized her. As if they were one and the same. When she was born, and her eyes turned from blue to a deep purple, her father mentioned how she was the heart of his life, like how the amethyst was the Heart of the court.

Grimot's body stiffened beside her, like a haunting thought had passed through him. But before she could blink, his body relaxed again.

"It's the exact one your mother found to win her Undertaking. The exact one your cohort will fight to find."

Kamine snorted. "I'm not trying to get to the Heart. I just want to keep my village safe."

"A noble thing."

"It's not my morals," Kamine conceded with little shame. "I think Roz would tear me to shreds if I tried to steal it from her."

He chuckled. "I wouldn't doubt it."

The soft sound of his breath rocked her. She wanted to hear him laugh again, and she wanted to be the cause of it.

"It's beautiful," she said, leaning in to inspect the glimmer of the purple gem. "How did it feel when your hand was on it, and you won?"

"Glorious. Like I was unstoppable. Like the future didn't matter because that moment was everything."

"Does it still feel that way?"

"No," he answered shortly.

Kamine turned to him, but his eyes were on the Heart. His expression was sullen. She dared to take his hand and give it a comforting squeeze.

"I think my mother felt the same. It's the tale they convince you to believe. That the Undertaking is a game, instead of a fight of survival."

"A game," he repeated after her. "One that so many will do unspeakable things to win. Things that they'll later regret."

Kamine didn't know exactly what he meant, but she could guess that he had his own demons when it came to his Undertaking.

"Do you ever wonder," he started, "if a part of you is holding back your powers because you're scared of what you'd do with them? That you might have a mental block?"

Kamine had considered that. She feared that if she had the power that her mother had, then she too would rather find the Heart instead of protecting her own.

"Not having control of my powers yet gives me something to focus on," she said. "I'm competing against myself, not the others."

"You really are noble," he responded, voice croaked with emotion.

"Thank you for showing me this," she said, gesturing to the stone with a smile. "I'll never forgive the Weather Gods for destroying my mother's spirit, but I do feel a little closer to her now."

They were still holding hands, but this time, he was the one who squeezed hers.

Fourteen

Kamine beamed with a new aura, Grimot thought, when at their next lesson, he tied her hands again. She had been the one to suggest it this time, claiming she wanted the challenge.

Perhaps being reminded of what she had lost, brought back everything that she still had yet to lose. Grimot could see the determination set in her purple eyes as she concentrated.

She had been standing there for almost an hour at this point, though he didn't rush or goad her. But Grimot began to wonder if it was time for him to step in.

He stepped forward, and she lifted her head to him.

"What if I can only make it work when I'm on the ground?"

"You're thinking too much still," he said. "The occasions where it worked, you weren't thinking about manifesting your powers. The first time, you were trying not to get hurt," his voice rasped. "The second time, you wanted to come around my fingers." He trailed those aforementioned fingers along her bare arms and she shivered.

"I think it's deeper than that," she admitted, breathily. "I think there was a truth to what you said last night. There's a block there because of my mother and what she represents to me."

"Is that so?" Grimot asked, as his fingers danced down her warm skin.

Kamine tilted her head back, as if savoring his touch, or willing herself to focus on her magic instead of him. He could tell she had failed, though, for when she looked at him, her pupils were dilated.

"That's a conversation for another time. Are you going to fuck me for real?" she goaded.

"I could..." he said against her ear. "A reward—only after you get your powers to surface."

"Well, then neither of us is leaving here happy."

He pulled her glasses from her face. Her mouth gaped open, but he shushed her. "Don't speak. Let's try upping the stakes. There is a high likelihood that you'll be knocked down during the Undertaking, and you won't be able to see if your glasses break."

She stiffened as the realization dawned on her. "I had never considered that."

He didn't step away. "What will you do?"

His mouth was so close to hers. He could feel her breath tickling his lips. He bent his head down and pressed a kiss to her neck.

She gasped. "That's cheating. I need to do this without you."

She was right. He wouldn't be there to coax her powers out during the Undertaking. But after yesterday, after she had spoken so freely to him about her past, he wanted to touch, and to comfort her.

He wanted her to know that he understood her pain. He wanted to tell her the truth about his own past—and he almost had. But he was worried she would look at him differently, and respect him less. Maybe once she completed her Undertaking, he would tell her. Because once this was over, Grimot knew he still wanted to spend his time with Kamine. That became clear last night, after she had poured her broken heart out to him. He wanted to make it whole again, piece by piece.

Grimot kissed the side of her lips.

"Professor," she breathed out.

His cock stirred, and he knew it was his sign to pull away.

"Get your powers to cooperate, and you can have me."

Kamine could barely see anything without her glasses. Everything in front of her was a blur. She focused on her breathing, not letting panic consume her.

She knew Grimot was somewhere in the room with her. She also knew that he was hard, and her mouth was practically salivating at the knowledge.

He was affected by her just as much as she was by him.

"Will you let me suck your cock if I do this?"

"Stop asking questions. You'll be alone during your Undertaking with no one to distract you, so don't try that as a strategy."

"The falling rocks will distract me," she said with a know-it-all tone.

"Rocks that will scare you," he pointed out. "Clear your mind. Remember, it's like moving a muscle."

Kamine rolled her eyes. "Just be careful with my glasses."

She adjusted her feet so that she was in a strong stance. She had taken off her shoes, giving her at least *some* direct contact with the ground. Grimot had pointed out that competing in the Undertaking without shoes wouldn't be ideal, but he allowed it for the sake of their practice.

Kamine evened her breathing and began to concentrate on a specific memory, one she thought about in fondness. This time, she thought about when she learned to swim. Her father had taken her and her mother out to a nearby lake. Kamine was only eight, and her mother floated in the water alongside Kamine and her father. Kamine's father held onto her outstretched hands, dragging her through the water. She kicked her little feet instinctually to stay afloat. She had been scared because she had to take her glasses off then, too. Her vision was poor, but her father used touch to reassure her, while her mother's words encouraged her to keep going. Kamine flailed her arms, but didn't swim anywhere at first, her body just trying to not drown. However, with her parents' guidance, she slowly learned to move forward. Years later, she could swim across the lake without rest.

Kamine let the survival skills that were innately part of her come to the surface. Her feet dipped as the ground beneath her swayed.

She reveled in the sensation, letting it continue. Her powers were hers to control. They were hers to decide when and how they manifested, just like her feet were hers. As the movement continued, Kamine tried taking a step forward. She didn't stumble, her body recognizing itself. She kept advancing towards the shadowy outline of Grimot that stood across from her.

When she reached him, he untied her hands, and she held them out. "Glasses."

"Don't you want your reward first?"

She cocked her head to the right, the ground becoming still, and a newfound boldness took over her body, as if her manifesting powers had shed a layer of doubt inside herself. "I want it on my own terms."

"And those are?"

Swallowing deeply, Kamine didn't allow herself to hesitate as she said, "I want you to fuck my mouth." The words felt strange on her tongue, yet they communicated exactly what she truly desired.

She noticed his posture straighten, and his pelvis brushed against her stomach. She felt his hardness, and her mouth watered at the promise of tasting him.

"It'll be more fun if you can't see," he suggested.

A shot of arousal went through her.

"Fine," she agreed, before glancing down at the glasses he still held hostage. "But put those somewhere safe."

Grimot stepped forward, backing her up, and Kamine could only follow him until she hit a wall.

"They'll be safe," he promised.

She heard a zip, but she placed her hands on his bulge to pause the action. "Let me."

Grimot removed his hand, and she undid the button, before pulling down his pants and underwear in one go. She wrapped her hand around him, feeling his solid length. As she rubbed his tip, she felt moisture beading.

She tightened the ponytail in her hair and dropped to her knees, then lapped at one side, then the next. Above her, Grimot hissed.

She sucked on the head, the taste of him exactly what she expected—strong and salty, something that would linger on her tongue for days. Kamine popped off his cock and licked her lips, staring at his glistening tip. "Do whatever you want," she said.

"Are you sure?" he asked, his voice wavering as she pumped him.

"Yes."

"Thank the Gods."

He pulled on her hair, and pain bolted across her scalp, though she found that she enjoyed it. He pushed himself in between her lips, crowding the back of her throat. She gagged, but urged him on. He kept going without abandon, her eyes watering, and her mouth drooling around him. Her hands fondled his balls as he thrust. Grimot moaned her name, and the sound made her want to touch herself, but this moment was about him. He had satisfied her, and now she needed to return the favor.

"Your mouth is so good," he murmured, his lips barely forming clear words. Kamine had a feeling he didn't even realize he was speaking out loud, and she loved that he was so disheveled, so willing to unleash himself so that she could please him thoroughly.

"I'm almost there," he grunted. He slid his hands around her throat, gently at first, as if asking permission. She coaxed them tighter, and he squeezed.

Kamine let her teeth drag against him, and she knew he liked it with the way his rhythm faltered, as he bucked and reached his peak, then exploded in her mouth.

Kamine took it all, and swallowed it down. When he had finished completely and pulled away, she wiped a dribble from the corner of her mouth, then licked her finger clean.

"Now we both can walk out of here happy," Kamine said with a smile. "I got my powers to work again, and you came so much, I thought I was going to choke on it."

He didn't say anything, just put her glasses on her so she could see him clearly. His face was devastated, as if he'd had the same realization she had when he'd gotten her off: no one else would ever compare.

"Who'd you fuck?" Janina asked bluntly as she distributed playing cards between herself and Zoya.

"What?" Kamine responded wide-eyed, trying her best to appear confused. The lesson had ended immediately after Grimot had finished, with both of them finding excuses as to why they had to leave. Kamine needed the distraction from the tender feelings bubbling up, so she naturally sought out her friends. Now she was realizing that was a mistake.

"Don't play coy." Janina's face twisted. "It wasn't Lycaster, was it?"

"No—"

"So it was *someone.*"

Zoya followed their conversation, her eyes bouncing between the two women.

"Why are you letting her grill me like this?" Kamine asked, sitting next to her colorful roommate, checking the hand of cards she was dealt.

Zoya shrugged. "I'm curious too. Though I have a guess."

Kamine poked her shoulder. "If you're so all-knowing, then who?"

"Professor Grimot," she said plainly, like it didn't shock or disturb her.

"That's insane. He's a Professor, and I'm a student."

"There's no rules prohibiting it."

No, there wasn't. With everyone trapped in this place, it was only inevitable that people started relying on one another to relieve the tension. Kamine had heard the rumors, like the night Janina had with Roz, and had actually once walked in on another couple mid-act in the bathing room. Apparently, so long as the coupling was consensual, no one at Skola seemed to mind. They all might be doomed anyways, if the Undertaking wasn't successful.

"You're blushing," Janina pointed out, her sharp fangs protruding as she smiled.

"Don't try to hide it. Just own it," Zoya said, as she placed her first card down.

"Fine," Kamine said. "But we're not just doing it for pleasure. We learned that I can access my powers this way, likely because I'm focused on other sensations beyond my powers."

"But it's still pleasurable?" Zoya asked, genuine concern knitting her brow..

"Yes, I found my pleasure."

"Then I think this is a good thing," Zoya said, satisfied.

Kamine wasn't so confident, but now that she'd had a taste of him, she couldn't get her mind off of her professor.

They'd pushed that boulder down the hill, and there was no way of stopping it.

✦

Fifteen

Days turned into weeks, and weeks turned into months.

Kamine had been giving it her all in her classes, and spent every other idle moment either hanging out with Janina and Zoya, or in private lessons with Grimot. Her friends supported her exploring this budding dynamic.

Grimot only allowed her to call him Professor when he was deep inside her. If she did it outside of that occasion, he would get hard in seconds. It was a fun trick sometimes, to walk by him in the halls and whisper that forbidden word. One time, when it was just the two of them, he'd pulled her into a small alcove, bent her over, and thrust right into her. She was at his mercy, and she had loved the lack of control, how she was at his whim. It was a nice reprieve from trying to control her own powers—which had strengthened considerably.

She could now wear her shoes, and also walk, as she made the ground beneath her bend to her will. She was even able to isolate her powers enough to shift a specific area more than the rest. Her body had also transformed with all the training and lifting. Sometimes Kamine looked at it proudly, sometimes tears fell because she feared she would hate the way she looked once she got out into the sunlit world, and could wear her dresses again.

Grimot staunched those fears by kissing every inch of her naked body.

Now, with it only being a week before the Undertaking, Kamine was especially anxious with anticipation for the big event.

The school always put on a showcase before the Undertaking, as a way for each student to demonstrate their skills, and everything they had learned. It was the morning of the showcase, but surprisingly, Kamine wasn't dreading it like she thought she would. Grimot had instructed her to keep her power under wraps, so that she could reveal her progress at the showcase. She found herself actually excited at the opportunity.

The best part? Her father and little brother were in attendance. All immediate family were invited to see the progress and give the participants one last hug or word of advice before the Undertaking. Damien had jumped and waved when he'd seen Kamine. She waved back, and caught a small pebble he had somehow thrown all the way to her. *His powers would one day change the world*, Kamine thought.

Lycaster stood at the center of the classroom with his hands in his pockets. He paced in a circle, slowly, dragging his feet. One second there was a pile of rocks behind him, the next he had thrown them to hit the center of five different targets. The crowd applauded.

Zoya went next. Her long hair was flowing down around her as she sat on the floor with her legs crossed. At first nothing happened; then rocks fluttered around her head and started weaving her hair into a braid. Once it reached the bottom, she tied it up. More applause.

And they kept going, until it was finally Kamine's turn.

Kamine entered the center of the room, the watchful eyes of familiar and unfamiliar faces grounded her to the here and now. The one benefit of just barely discovering her powers was that she didn't need to do anything flashy. Grimot told her to keep it simple, a small movement would cause a rumble in the crowd.

She cracked her neck and waited. She wanted to build suspense. Janina and Zoya held hands, as if they anticipated their whole world spinning.

It was a loud silence, but Kamine's mind calmed as she let that mental wall down. One second everything was standing still, and the next, a gasp split through the crowd as the vibrations built beneath Kamine's feet. Rocks tumbled off their pedestals and crashed to the classroom floor.

Then, concentrating, Kamine quieted the world again. A roar of applause hit as everyone got their bearings again. The entire cohort all congratulated her. Zoya presented her with the knitted blanket—the colors vibrant, just like Kamine had expected it to be. The entire affair was joyous, and carefree.

Damien ran towards her on his wobbly feet, and handed her a dandelion weed he must have picked at some point before arriving at Skola. She bent down and accepted it, and pressed a quick kiss to his cheek that he immediately rubbed off. She laughed. Her father came up to her with a tear in his eye, and hugged her tightly.

She knew he had been nervous about her participation in the Undertaking from the beginning, even if he would never admit it. Now, alongside his fear, she could also sense his pride.

"I love you," he whispered in her ear. "I'm so proud, and she would have been so excited for you."

"I love you, too," she said, ignoring the second half of his words. She didn't know if she believed them.

She twisted the bracelet on her hands, unable to look her father in the eye. Sensing her discomfort, her father jerked his head towards the hallway, and she followed him.

Headmistress Dritoria was holding Damien, and she nodded her acknowledgement as the both of them left. Grimot narrowed his eyes at Kamine, concerned, but she waved at him, letting him know she was okay.

Her father weaved through the halls with ease, and Kamine had forgotten that once he was a student that had learned to navigate them, too.

They found a secluded room, where her father sat down, then patted the seat next to him.

"What's wrong?" she asked, worried that he had bad news to share.

"Nothing." He shook his head, his brown shaggy hair bouncing as he did. "I wanted to tell you a story. *The* story of my, and your mother's, Undertaking."

Kamine swallowed, completely unprepared for this moment. For years, Kamine had pestered her father to tell her what happened during their Undertaking. Every time, he refused, revealing that he promised his wife that he would keep it a secret. Kamine learned long ago to stop expecting any answers. That fact that he was finally willing to spill the truth now meant something big.

"Our Undertaking was like any other. The cohort was separated to each of their villages to defend it. As expected, some participants chose to find the Heart. I chose to run to mine—your mother." Her father cleared his throat, and Kamine rubbed his shoulder. "We were from neighboring villages, so I was still able to defend my people as I ran. On my way to her, a rock blasted from behind me, and knocked me to the ground. I was struck unconscious until your mother found me and shook me awake. I was bleeding badly. Your mother was trying to comfort me, but the pain was unbearable, and I was losing a lot of blood. No one had yet found the Heart, so rocks continued to rain down. Your mother left me to find it herself, to put an end to the Undertaking, so I could get help. I told her to not go, because with me injured, our people needed someone to defend both of our villages. She refused to listen."

Kamine took in his words, a deep ache opening in her chest at the difficult circumstance they had endured.

"She found it quickly. I have no idea how, perhaps the Gods took mercy on us, but even her speed did not end the Undertaking before her family was killed."

Kamine's world halted, and her ears began to ring with the shock of her father's admission. "What?" she breathed out.

"Your mother was never the same because of it. She believed herself unworthy of living." True tears spilled down her father's face. "I tried convincing her otherwise. I tried reminding her that it wasn't her fault. But it wasn't enough."

Her father pulled back her sleeve to reveal the gold bracelet that Kamine had such difficulty parting with. He slid his finger over it, feeling the ridges of the small gold leaves that created a long, never-ending vine. "Your mother craved life. That's why whenever she was pregnant, she came back to herself again. That's why I gave her the reminder on her wrist that there was a whole living world outside."

"That's why she always looked out the window," Kamine finished.

Her father nodded. "She loved you so much, Kamine. I understand why you might not believe that to be true, but she did. When she decided to leave this world, she left this bracelet for you, so you would always have that reminder of her, and to keep living when she no longer could herself."

Kamine didn't cry, only stared at the bracelet on her wrist.

Her father pulled her into his chest, and she let him, offering him the little comfort she could while accepting the little comfort he offered.

The tunnels were the same, but different. The dark walls hadn't changed—they were still lifeless and barren. Each step through led her to the same locations she had learned to navigate. The difference was in her.

No longer did she view Skola as a trap. It was instead a dungeon, before an inevitable execution. One that each of them—and every village—accepted it to be.

Her mother, even as determined as she was to protect her village, still left this place a shell because of the decisions she had made. Every participant who had been voted in, and entered Skola ready to restore the power of the court, left with something taken from them. All in the name of the Weather Gods.

When Kamine made it back to her room, Janina and Zoya were already there, asleep on the ground, tangled in Zoya's yarn. The burst of colors were a stark contrast to the rest of their surroundings, and it was another reminder of everything they had to lose.

At the sight, a loud sob escaped Kamine. Both her friends awoke at her cry, immediately scanning for the source of the sound. When their eyes landed on her, their faces softened.

Kamine fell to her knees, the plush rug and her friends catching her, and crawled between them.

Kamine finally weeped for the mother that had been taken from her.

The anger she had held for her mother now turned to guilt, a feeling that coated her skin. For years, Kamine could barely spare her mother a kind word because of the rage that brewed deep inside her. An anger that had been unjust.

"We're here," Zoya whispered.

The words only caused Kamine to cry harder, as a fear for the future of her friends mixed with the storm of emotions surfacing. She had no idea if her friends even knew why she was crying, but she appreciated them for simply understanding that she needed them.

"She deserved better," Kamine sobbed. And she wasn't just talking about the Undertaking, and what it had taken from her mother. She deserved a daughter who would have been more understanding. Not Kamine, who only grew to resent her mother's emptiness, until it festered into such a blockage it stopped her powers from fully manifesting.

"You both deserved better," Zoya responded, rubbing her back.

Janina pulled a blanket off Kamine's bed, and draped it over all of them. From her pocket, she pulled out a bag of sugared nuts from the reception. "Sugar usually helps me."

Kamine's mouth gaped at the simplicity of the offer, and the beauty of it. How even in the darkest times, her friends' light could so effortlessly comfort by just being there. It would be a long time before she untangled every coursing thought running through her, but as she lay there with her friends, she had no doubt it was possible to find the other side and thrive.

Kamine snatched the bag from Janina, saying, "Thank the Weather Gods—at least they are good at creating *something*."

All of them laughed, and Kamine thought that the sound was joyous enough to shake all of the shadows from the world.

Sixteen

Janina's smelly foot in Kamine's face luckily woke her up, otherwise, Kamine didn't think she would have managed to make it to her final lesson with Grimot on time.

He was waiting outside the classroom, and pulled her in for a sweet kiss.

Kamine wrapped an arm around his neck as their kiss deepened, their bodies fusing. Her foot kicked up as he overwhelmed her in the best way, like she was in the middle of a raging storm, with everything soaked, a dizzying chill settled in her bones.

When they pulled apart, she asked, "What was that for?"

He shrugged. "I just sensed you needed it."

Kamine swallowed, taking him in. This man who once angered her endlessly was now the source of so much peace for her. She pet his cheek, trailing her fingers down to his beard.

They held each other's gaze, her eyes focusing and unfocusing, not allowing herself to blink. Each time, she came back to the clarity of those dark eyes that pierced her soul.

"We have a lesson we need to do."

She scoffed. "Maybe we can skip it?" She dragged her fingers across his lips.

"No," he growled, biting the tip of finger, then pushing himself away. "You need to recenter yourself. I know something happened after the reception with your father. I saw you running away with tears."

Kamine touched her bracelet, and he followed the movement.

"Life. The source of my power is remembering there is life beyond death."

Grimot stepped up to her, lifted her wrist to his mouth and kissed one of the gold leaves. Her pulse jumped in response.

"I've always had a connection with the earth in a way I could never explain. After speaking with my father, after he told me what my mother did during her Undertaking, it all clicked."

To prove that her powers now came to her seamlessly, she rippled and dipped the ground under Grimot until she was taller than him.

He smiled up at her. "I'm jealous. Your powers are better than mine."

She rolled her eyes and evened out the ground upon which he stood. As she looked at him, an ache pressed in her chest, and she knew what it meant. They were words she couldn't voice quite yet, afraid of what it would mean for the two of them.

"Meet me tonight in my room," he said, his voice going low enough that she felt it in her gut.

She nodded in agreement.

That lesson, Grimot forced her to go through drills to hone her already impressive skills further. They played with her powers, discovering new and creative ways for Kamine to protect her village. He pushed her until she was confident in her abilities, until she could go into the Undertaking prepared, and ready to truly make her mother proud. Every rock she stopped from killing her people would be for the woman who loved her father so deeply that she destroyed herself for it. Kamine now understood what type of courage that took.

Grimot opened the door right as Kamine prepared to knock. He gasped at the sight of her. Her braids from earlier were now down, letting her curls run wild. She had changed out of her training clothes into a simple off-white dress that hugged her chest and flowed out around her hips, accentuating her waist.

She dipped her head shyly as he inspected her.

He could kiss her right there and now, but he wouldn't get distracted from his goal.

"Let's go," he said, taking her hand in his. Her fingers were calloused now from all the training, and he savored that feeling when it was around his cock, but he loved it even more as they rubbed against his palm. There was an innate intimacy to hand-holding that he never realized before. It was a comforting balm against his ragged soul.

"I hope you're not taking me to another torturous game where I almost die."

"Nothing like that," he responded. He guided her through the tunnels as they ventured up, up, up.

She groaned behind him. He could feel the fatigue radiating off her, but hopefully the destination would be worth the climb. He knew from the moment that she had mentioned her powers were sourced from her connection with the living that he needed to bring her here. He needed to share this place with her.

They eventually reached a tall ladder that Grimot slowly climbed while swearing at the pain in his legs, where at the top, he lifted up a door. A sharp intake of breath sounded from behind him.

"Won't we get in trouble?" she asked, worry lining her brow.

He didn't say anything, instead climbed back down and gestured for her to go up. She hesitated, but did as instructed, and he followed right behind her.

When he lifted himself out, Kamine already had her chin tilted up, her eyes on the night sky, glittering with stars. She raised her arms, as if reaching for them, the bracelet on her wrist gleaming in the moonlight as if it too missed the outdoors.

"It's beautiful," she breathed.

He stared right at her as he said, "It is."

She closed her eyes. "It's been so long since I've had fresh air on my skin."

Grimot stood at the edge of the mountain, taking in the sight before him. There wasn't much to see, but from a distance, he could just make out a small village. The lights of homes flickered, just like the stars above them.

Grimot pulled a basket from behind a large rock, and laid down a soft blanket.

"What's this?" she asked, her eyes widening.

He popped a bottle of sparkling wine. "A congratulations."

She narrowed her eyes. "This isn't over yet. I still have the actual Undertaking to survive."

Pouring two glasses, he handed her one, then clinked their glasses together. "You still deserve it."

He beckoned her to join him on the blanket. She did, and leaned her head against his shoulder.

Everything was so different with her than it had been with Kestra. Sure, both women had made him satisfied in bed, but with Kamine, he craved *more*. Not only of her body—which he loved each inch of—but of her mind and soul.

"I can feel you thinking." Her words rumbled against him.

"I'm thinking of you."

"Great thoughts to have."

He chuckled and he wrapped his arms around her to bring her closer. He kissed the top of her head.

They sat there, just existing in each other's presence. He reflected on the past few months, and the joy it brought him. Even on days where he woke up with his knees and elbows stiffer, when the dread of the curse consumed him, he thought of Kamine and the worries fluttered away, like pages flipping in a book.

Then, Kamine started rubbing his thigh, which made him drag his fingers up and down her back, which led to her unzipping his pants, then taking him in her mouth.

He pulled her chin away from him and laid her down so she could stare at the sky while he fucked her. He unbuttoned the front of her dress, kissing her skin as he went, revealing his favorite curls. When she was fully bare, and the chill of the air caused her skin to pebble, he took off his own clothes, and put his body on hers. He slid into her slowly, taking his time to go deep, to that spot he knew would have her writhing. While his one hand rubbed her clit, the other leveraged his body weight to hover above her.

She cupped the back of his neck and brought him down to her, kissing him, nipping at his lips as he rocked in and out. She pressed her mouth to those two stones in his clavicle, savoring everything they represented. As she wrapped her legs around him to anchor her hips up so that he hit her even deeper, she moaned loudly, unafraid of the world below them, or of the Gods above them, hearing.

It was just the two of them. No past, no future, just the present where their two bodies collided, creating a rumble across the land that would be felt forever in their souls.

Seventeen

They lay on their backs, enjoying the night air on their sweaty, exposed skin. Grimot dragged his fingers up and down her navel, a whisper of a touch, memorizing every mole on her pale flesh. They were more beautiful than the stars above; she was the most beautiful thing he'd ever seen.

"I never want to leave," she confessed.

Grimot smiled—truly smiled—because he never wanted her to leave either. He wanted her next to him forever. He wanted to wake up with her each morning, and fall asleep with her each night. With the way she talked, perhaps that future would be possible, or perhaps Grimot was delusional. He still had a lot of apologizing to do.

He rested on his side, anchoring his elbow under his head to really look at her.

"I'm sorry for traumatizing you on that first day," he said. He was so blinded by his pent up anger and the pressure of his own success that he'd taken it out on her. It hadn't been fair, and he hated that he had allowed those emotions to cause him to be so cruel.

She bit her lip, as if reliving the moment, and how she had been humiliated in front of everyone. "You really were such an asshole to me, but I think the most traumatizing part was you calling me Kammy." She gagged, theatrically. "Be grateful I never called you Grim."

He shuddered at the sound of that nickname that only Kestra had ever used, one he hated even back then. "I'm very grateful." He brushed a piece of her hair behind her ear. "And I am truly sorry." The words would never be enough, but one day, he hoped he would prove how guilty he felt.

"I forgive you," she said. "Only because of the great orgasms."

His heart raced as he asked, "Is that the only reason you keep coming back? Because of the sex?"

She pondered his question for a moment, and Grimot swallowed down the bile rising in his throat.

"Maybe at first, but I don't think so anymore," she finally admitted.

"Good, because I like you for more than just the sex, too."

A flash of lighting, and a growl of thunder sounded somewhere in the distance. Growing up, he'd loved thunderstorms. The loudness of it, the anticipation of when light would streak the sky. After his Undertaking, he resented storms for a long time. They reminded him of how desperately he had reached for a goal, only to be left unsatisfied afterwards. It was the rush of the game, just like Kamine had mentioned.

Tonight, though, he breathed a sigh of relief that his childhood ache for the power of the storms was back. It made him whole again.

"What else do you like about me?" she crooned.

He contemplated, but the answer was easy. "I like that you're scared, but you don't let that fear stop you. You're determined and strong-willed. I like that you would rather be reading a book in your room than showing off your strength or powers. You're brilliant and kind. Forgiving, too."

Kamine blinked rapidly, and his heart ached at watching her become emotional at such simple words that poured from his mouth.

He palmed one of her breasts to lighten the mood. "These are great, too though."

She laughed, her head tipping back. "Can't forget about those."

He kissed her passionately, hoping to convey the emotions that he could not properly voice.

Their kiss broke and Grimot started, "Before you—"

"What's this?" a voice yelped from behind them.

They both jolted, but Grimot shifted to shield Kamine with his own body.

"The two of you seem comfortable," Kestra said, jealousy lining her harsh voice.

"Leave, Kestra," Grimot shot back. The shock of her presence had worn off. "There's no reason for you to be here."

"And what's your reason? To fuck her?"

He growled. "Go."

"Poor thing..." Kestra said directly to Kamine, who was hiding under the blanket, her body shivering. "Being the second woman he uses." Kestra offered a sickly smile while Kamine's brow creased with confusion. Before Grimot could interject, Kestra said, "He didn't tell you?"

"Shut it!" he yelled.

"She deserves to know, Grim. What kind of a cheat and a failure you actually are."

"Not like this," he whispered. He had planned to tell her. He just wanted to do it on his own terms, when he felt ready and solid in...whatever this was between the two of them.

Kestra paced to the edge of the mountain. "Before you, Grim fucked *me*." Grimot felt Kamine flinch beside him, and the sensation made him want to turn around and hold her, to comfort her. "I hide the Heart each year as the Gods intend, so I know exactly where it will be. Grim knew that, so he slept with me to learn the location before his Undertaking."

As Kestra kept talking, Kamine pulled further and further away from Grimot.

Kestra continued, but Grimot imagined kicking her over the edge to get her to stop speaking. "He was so desperate for glory and attention, he would do anything for it. He won his Undertaking because he cheated, and now the Weather Gods have cursed him." She turned around. "That's why he's here. Doing this will put him back on the good side of the Gods. That's why he took you under his wing. Not because he loves you, but because you're someone he could fix for his own gain. A good deed."

Kamine's eyes began to glisten, and Grimot could practically feel the way her heart broke at Kestra's words.

"That's not—" But the words died on his lips, because he was tired of lying. Part of what Kestra said was true, and there was no running away from it. Kamine deserved to know it all, every broken, jagged part of him.

"Enjoy these last moments together." Kestra said cheerily, satisfied with the chaos she caused. "You'll soon part ways, and forget each other."

Then, she left.

Kamine quickly got up, gathering her clothes. She was like her own storm with the way she frantically swirled around. He got up to follow her, not caring that he was still naked.

"Kamine, wait!" He tried taking her hand. He wanted to stop her, to kiss her, to tell her that while his actions may have started one way, what this had progressed to was so much more.

She pulled away. "Don't touch me," her voice cracked. "I want nothing to do with you."

"Don't say that." He couldn't bear hearing such words from her lips, not when minutes before she admitted that what she felt went beyond physicality.

She was muttering under her breath, calling herself a stupid fool for trusting him. She whipped around, as if she finally got the courage to face him. "How could you!" She yelled, tears now tracking down her cheek.

He opened his mouth, but she stopped him.

"I was nothing more than your experiment!"

"No."

"You're a piece of shit liar," she said with such force that he stumbled backwards, accidentally knocking over one of the wine glasses. It shattered.

The storm that was in the distance was nearing. He reminded himself that all storms eventually passed. This one would be the same. It had to be. Because otherwise, what was the point? Nothing before Kamine had mattered—not even winning his Undertaking had been as important to him then as she was to him now.

"Was everything you said even the truth, or just a way to make me feel better about myself so I could perform well during my Undertaking?"

"Of course it was the truth!"

She shook her head, her hair a wild mess. "I couldn't even believe you if I wanted to." She pulled her shoes on and walked away.

This time, he let her go.

Eighteen

The last few days before everything would change had passed. Kamine had gone to her classes, enjoyed meals with her friends, and reread her books—but she did not seek out Grimot. She avoided him completely.

Janina and Zoya had relayed to her that he wanted a chance to explain himself. He had pulled her friends aside from class and practically begged them to help him connect with her. Kamine refused to listen. Her friends respected that decision, and even agreed with it when Kamine finally explained to them the truth about what he had done. They were angry for her, but Kamine had an underlying suspicion they still hoped that she would take the chance to listen to Grimot explain his side of things. As if they, like her, realized that he had changed her for the better. She kept telling herself that their time together wasn't completely pointless. He did help her bring out her powers.

But Kamine felt betrayed, and no amount of words would alleviate that. She also couldn't allow him to get in the way of her training. She needed every second remaining to prepare to face the

Undertaking, and she wouldn't waste it brooding over a man who had used her for his own gain.

"I think we're officially the strongest cohort yet," Zoya said, as she devoured her last meal before the Undertaking.

Kamine pushed around the mush of food with her fork, unable to stomach it. Her nerves had reached new heights, as if she were standing atop a cliff with nothing to catch her if she fell. What if she couldn't save her village? What if something happened to her family?

"No one is as strong as me," Roz replied from another table in the dining hall.

"We'll let tomorrow be the judge of who's the strongest," Janina added under her breath.

Everyone else in the room reserved their energy, and kept to themselves. The anticipation for tomorrow had built up to a high, a palpable atmosphere that Kamine could almost drown in.

"You should talk to him."

Kamine whipped her head up to Zoya, the sudden movement causing her neck to crack. "What?"

Her friend shrugged. "You'll regret it, especially if something happens tomorrow."

"He doesn't deserve any more of my time."

"Maybe not, but you deserve the truth. There's more to the story."

Kamine scoffed. That man was insufferable and gross. She was naïve to have ever believed that he had good intentions when he practically demanded to assist her. Her emotions had been high from the moment she stepped into the school, and he took advantage of that to break a curse that existed because of his selfish past actions.

But a part of her thought Zoya was right. She deserved to know why. When Kamine heard what Kestra revealed about Grimot's past, Kamine's heart had shattered. Kamine had her own sexual history, so it wasn't that Grimot had slept with Kestra that made what she revealed hard to swallow. It was that Grimot cared so much for the glory that he would do anything for it. He would have rather cheat the game than win with honor.

Kamine couldn't intrinsically understand a person like that. She never could. But, Kamine had to remind herself that everything wasn't so black and white. What her mother had done had hurt Kamine endlessly, but that didn't ultimately mean her mother hadn't still loved her child. The same way that although Grimot's actions pained her, it didn't automatically mean that his feelings for her weren't still strong and true. Even if his motives had been intentionally false, perhaps his feelings had changed once he'd spent more time with her, just like her own opinions of him had changed as he opened up his heart to her. Still, she had a right to be afraid of trusting him again.

"What if I don't want to hear what he has to say?" she asked.

Janina said, "Then you don't have to. You could decide to go to his room and throw rocks at him, just like he did to you, and we would support you. We'd even join you."

A small smile broke across Kamine's lips. She would never be more grateful to have the two of them during the hardest months of her life. She wouldn't have survived this journey without them. They were her rock. Just like Grimot had become.

Kamine pulled off her glasses and rubbed the tiredness from her eyes. "Alright, I'll go," she announced unceremoniously. Her friends cheered her on as she left the echoes of the dining hall.

Emotions slammed into Kamine as she searched the halls, just like when Grimot had thrown rocks at her, each one hitting her in different parts of her body. Her head spun with exhaustion, her muscles ached, and her heart weighed heavily in her chest.

"He's not here," Headmaster Dritoria said as she came out of her office.

Kamine blinked, trying to make sense of the words. The realization that the Headmaster knew of her budding relationship with Grimot made her blush. She opened her mouth to explain herself, but Headmaster Dritoria put her hands up.

"I don't want to know. You're both adults who can make decisions for yourselves." Headmaster Dritoria sighed. "He left to go back to his village so he can be with his people and family. All the professors do."

Kamine nodded. That made sense. It wouldn't be fair that the professors got to stay safely in the school while the rest of the court needed to face the horrors of the Undertaking.

"He looked devastated," Headmaster Dritoria admitted. "I've only seen him look that way one time before. It's when he came here and begged for a job."

Kamine couldn't see it, if she were honest. Grimot was always so sure of himself. It was hard to believe that he truly thought he was cursed.

"He told me that ever since his Undertaking, ever since he won, he hadn't felt the same. That seemed to change when he was with you."

Kamine gulped. She doubted she had such an impact on him.

"I was scared when he came to me," the Headmaster added. "His curse was damning. I couldn't say no."

The curse. Kamine had been too scared to ask what it was. With him gone, though, she needed to know. "What is his curse?"

Headmaster Dritoria's shoulders slumped. "His body is to turn to stone if your cohort fails, or if any of you cheat."

Kamine felt the blood rush from her head, and her body swayed. She steadied herself against the wall, as her body became weightless with the truth.

"The Weather Gods are a cruel sort," Kamine said with fervor, her voice filled with anger.

"Yet we must play their game," Headmaster Dritoria responded.

Kamine's whole body wanted to lay down and never get up, forget about the Undertaking, and tell the Gods to fuck themselves—but she still had more that needed done. For her mother, she would do it. For her father and brother. For Grimot, whose life now depended on the entire cohort. She wouldn't give up that easily. The Undertaking had become more than just a competition for her. It had become her way of defying all expectations.

Nineteen

Fierce winds whipped biting strands of her hair across her face. A drizzling rain had started as soon as she arrived, and the ground was becoming slick, but Kamine couldn't focus on anything but what lay in front of her.

Her village hadn't changed since she left, as if it had frozen in time, waiting for her arrival. The stores were locked up for the day, everyone at home with their loved ones in case they didn't make it out, because hiding in any type of bunker would be considered cheating, and no one wanted to anger the Weather Gods. Her own family was likely sheltering together in one room. Kamine hoped Damien didn't cry. She hoped she could prevent death today, that every last one of her villagers would make it out alive.

She hoped Grimot was safe in his home, surrounded by his family.

Kamine had spent the whole night pondering what she would tell him when she saw him again, because she *would* see him again. There was no alternative.

Others in her cohort spent the night praying to the Gods led by Kestra. Kamine didn't bother. She refused to get on her knees for the Gods, and she didn't dare approach Kestra.

A horn blasted loudly, and Kamine's first instinct was to duck and run to safety—but the gravity of the moment hit her. Today, she was the one to keep others safe. The others depended on *her*.

Her clothes clung to her body uncomfortably as they dampened, and her protective armor was heavy with the rain. She breathed deeply through her nose to calm herself.

She thought about her parents and how years ago they were in a similar position as her. She thought about every past Undertaking participant facing this harrowing reality. If she survived this—*when* she survived, she tried convincing herself—she would become part of a legacy. One that would either destroy her completely, or remind her to keep living each day to its fullest.

In the distance, the first rock fell. Kamine softened its fall as it landed in a large open field, and then let the ground swallow it. Another rock came before she blinked. It rolled down a hill, headed straight for the main square. Kamine split the ground in two and watched as the rock disappeared before it could cause any damage.

A shower of rocks came next, small ones that she had to ignore to focus on the larger ones, even if it hurt to watch them destroy the roofs of homes. Already, Kamine's energy began to wane. She didn't know how long she would last, but she would fight every second that she could.

Her abilities limited how much she could actually do. She wasn't able to stop a rock midair like some of the others, or crush the rocks with her mind. She learned to get creative where she could.

One large boulder was barreling directly for someone's home. She used her powers to move the land underneath the building, until it was out of the way. The rock smashed into a dirt mount beside the home, the rubble exploding with the impact. Kamine stumbled slightly, regaining her balance once the ground stilled again.

Yet, the storm of rocks did not stop. With every rock that she managed to move out of the way, Kamine tried to take a deep breath, but there was no break from the onslaught of the Undertaking.

She wondered how anyone—how Grimot—could abandon their people just to find the Heart. The image in front of her was too horrifying to even think about winning the Undertaking. To her, winning would be seeing her village safe.

Grimot regretted it, Kamine reminded herself. Watching her mother take her own life was proof enough that her mother couldn't exist with the knowledge that people died because of her, even if she had pursued the Heart to save her one true love. The Weather Gods might call it cowardly, but Kamine considered it human.

Humans were never meant to come to terms with killing others, intentionally or not.

Kamine had become so focused on the barrage in front of her that she didn't notice a rock coming down from behind. The force of it knocked her face down, and her glasses flew off her face. The blurring in her eyes raged as she tried to lift herself up, but her body became incapable of movement, her limbs stuck. She heard a terrible crash, and Kamine's heart jolted inside her, terrified of what and who the rock might have hit. She didn't let the panic sweep in—she thought instead of the past, thought of the good times with her family as she strained to push herself up.

She spit the dirt that got into her mouth, and assessed her body. Nothing was broken, but her protective gear had dented on her right leg. She crawled around, feeling the earth until cold metal bit into her skin. Sliding her glasses onto her face, she inspected what had occurred.

The onslaught of rocks seemed to slow down. Either the Gods were giving her mercy or false hope. She used that time to wander towards her home, a slight limp in her gait. Right as she began trekking down the hill, careful not to slip on the slick mud, a flash of pink raced by her.

"Watch it," Roz gritted out. She ran quickly, no armor covering her at all. Was she that confident in herself?

Kamine watched Roz, who kept her eyes open and searched every area around her. Behind stacks of hay, under wheelbarrows that held mountains of rooted vegetables, and even inside an abandoned barn. Each time she came back empty-handed, and Kamine could feel the frustration radiating off her.

Kamine skidded to a halt next to a fountain in the town's square. "No luck in your village with the Heart?" Roz's village neighbored Kamine's, making it easier to get here than the others, but she expected that the rest of her cohort would be showing up, too.

Roz shook her head, her breaths heavy with exhaustion, but didn't let her eyes stray away from her goal. She kicked over small rocks on the ground, and pushed aside sacks of grain.

"And you think it's here?"

Roz nodded without a word, determined to accomplish her goal.

"Why?"

Roz sighed as she stopped what she was doing to turn towards her. "Because of how close you and Professor Grimot had become."

Another figure bounded towards them. "Did you find it?" Lycaster asked as he rested his hands on his knees, taking labored breaths.

Kamine didn't know what to make of everyone flocking here. Wouldn't the Heart be hidden somewhere important? Kamine never considered her village to be special. Kamine just knew that her mother found the Heart hidden in a cave, a few villages over.

Janina and Zoya now jogged to the group. Kamine immediately inspected her friends, and besides a gash on Zoya's cheek, they both were uninjured.

"You too?" Kamine asked.

They shrugged. "It seemed like the obvious place," they said in unison.

Kamine crossed her arms. "It's not like I cheated and had Kestra place the Heart here to make it easier for me." She would never dare test the Gods that way, even if she believed that they almost encouraged such behavior, so they could punish someone. The Gods *would* be that manipulative.

"Maybe not," Zoya said. "But the Gods would tell her to place it here. Somewhere it will hurt."

Kamine supposed there was some sense to that assumption. The Weather Gods wouldn't just make it hard to find the Heart, but also emotionally difficult. Kamine was also the easiest to target, with her past being so tied to this harrowing, yearly event.

"I—" But Kamine stopped herself. She suddenly knew exactly where it would be. Somewhere that she had avoided for years. Kamine didn't utter a word before she sprinted off.

Being back home after months away had been disorienting. Everything around Grimot seemed to have changed. His favorite bakery had closed because the owner had died, the tree that he loved climbing on as a child had been cut down, and his room had turned into a nursery. His mother discovered she was unexpectedly pregnant while he was gone. A welcomed surprise, his mother mentioned, especially at her older age of forty-five. A blessing from the Gods, she muttered.

His parents welcomed him back with open arms, but this home no longer had the same sensation of comfort and ease. All these changes weighed on him, because the world kept moving even if he wasn't around.

He had no purpose, no direction. He had nothing to wake up for everyday. The one good thing he had was ripped away because his past decisions once again haunted, and found him, and ruined it. He had lost her.

Look at me now, he thought. He stared at himself in the freshly cleaned mirror, his mother's doing no doubt, and barely recognized himself. His shoulder-length hair was down. He had a pair of scissors in his hands, ready to cut that unbearable history off him. His hands refused to move, his body becoming stiffer as each rock and boulder rained down around them. He could sense it in his fingertips that he would soon become a statue, lost to time.

He should be hiding somewhere, staying safe. He could hear the pounding of the rocks coming down at full force on the roof. Grimot trusted Zoya, though. She was the chosen protector of Grimot's village, and Zoya was skilled with her powers. He selfishly hoped Kamine had followed her own desires to stay put, and protect her own instead of dooming herself to any regret.

He huffed, and sat down in the old rocking chair, one his mother used when he was a babe. It creaked under him.

A shudder rocked through the house. He clenched the arms of the chair. His hands would miss Kamine's supple skin. His heart would miss the way she bit her lip as she read her book, or how she smiled at her friends with such open adoration.

He should go be with his parents. He should go make sure his mother was calm, and safe. But as he pulled himself up, one of his arms would not budge as it stuck to the chair. He yanked, but he hissed at the excruciating pain, as his body began to turn to stone and graft into the chair. He opened his mouth to scream for help, but the roof came down on him.

Twenty

The others were on her heels, but Kamine barely noticed their footfalls past the plummeting rocks. A boulder came down towards them but before Kamine could react, Janina threw it away. The others watched the skies closely for the next one.

As Kamine neared the cemetery, she used her powers to shake the ground behind her. She heard the others yell as they fell to the ground. It wasn't that she was desperate to win, she just needed a moment to collect herself.

She skidded to a stop at the entrance. The headstones peeked from the earth, each of them a symbol of a soul lost. Many of them were cracked, but her mother's headstone barely had a scratch. Fresh-cut flowers surrounded the stone—likely her father and Damien had visited.

"Oh," Zoya quietly said, as she bounded up to where Kamine stood. She rested her hand on Kamine's shoulder. "Do you need some time alone? I can hold them off."

Kamine could barely muster a nod, but Zoya ran off. Kamine dragged herself to her mother's grave, and fell to her knees. As she slammed down, the world bent with her. Grunts sounded behind her again, and she winced at the unintentional use of her powers.

"I made it," she whispered to her mother's stone. "I'm here protecting our people. I'm keeping our family safe."

The wind blew by, settling into her hair and patting her cheek—an assuring gesture just like her mother had done when she had pulled Kamine out from under her bed during that Undertaking, and brought her in close. Her own mother put her fears aside to comfort her child as she rubbed her fingers into Kamine's scalp to relax her.

Kamine now caressed her own fingers over the rough stone.

"I hope you're proud of me. I hope that you found peace." Kamine sniffled, and wiped at her nose. "I think I finally found mine."

That revelation, that truth, freed Kamine from so much of her resentment. She could let it go now. It had never served her, anyway. A part of Kamine would always find what her mother did painful. It would always make Kamine sad that she never experienced the woman that her father had first fallen in love with, but she didn't need to keep that pain so close anymore. She picked up a weathered rock, and let her hurt and sorrow flow into it; then she smashed it into dust.

"I miss you so much," she said through her tears. "But I'm going to bring home the light that was taken from you. I promise."

"Kamine!" someone yelled from behind her. She was shoved to the side. She didn't even care who did it. She understood that the others were on a mission for the Heart, and she was just a block in the road.

Franciz circled the headstone. "I don't see it."

Roz reached them, her usual pristine hair whipped into a complete mess. "Do you think we have to dig?"

Kamine swallowed down the acid bubbling in her chest. Could she allow them to disrupt her mother's resting place? Could she allow *herself* to do it?

Then she thought of Kestra, the one responsible for hiding the Heart. She would do something like this. Although that wasn't a fair assessment of the situation, Kamine knew that the Weather Gods had told her where to place it. Perhaps Kamine was cursed, then, too.

"Let's dig," Kamine decided.

The whole cohort had arrived it seemed. The others kneeled down beside her and used their hands to cup the soil, and pull it away. With eight of them, they worked quickly. The hole grew larger. Zoya stopped at some point to focus her attention on any oncoming rocks.

"Anything?" Magda gritted through their teeth. Their hands were caked in mud. Kamine's own clotted fingernails made her cringe.

"Not yet," Janina said. Kamine could tell that she was getting frustrated.

"If we keep going," Zoya interjected, "we'll hit the casket."

"Somewhere it'll hurt, right?" Kamine said, defeated. Silently, she apologized to her mother.

Kamine outstretched her arms and began digging again. The others followed, allowing her to take the lead. With each stroke, Kamine got closer to facing a reality she had ignored for so long. Even during her burial, Kamine didn't dare look at the wooden box. She had stared at her hands the whole time. She had refused to accept it, because she was so angry at her mother. How could she leave her family? How could her mother not face the choices she had made?

Maybe the Weather Gods were offering her a second chance at something she regretted.

Roz hit something on her side of the hole. "We're close."

They all quickened their pace. The wood had barely decayed.

"You should open it," Janina said to Kamine.

Kamine bit her lip, unsure if she could take that final step, but if she didn't, one of the others would.

Kamine reached down and grabbed the handle. The door wouldn't budge at first; the hinges were rusted. She pulled and pulled, but it still wouldn't give. She had no idea how Kestra had gotten inside if it was in there, but Kamine wouldn't question the Gods' methods. Franciz stepped in and tried to help. With more force, they heard the wood crack around the lock.

Kamine took a deep breath and pulled it open. The stench hit her first. Kamine gagged, and the sight of her mother's dead body made her stomach twist and seize.

A storm of small rocks began raining down.

"We need to hurry," Zoya said. "It's going to start again."

"I see it," Roz said, excitedly. Then her demeanor changed. "I see it, and I don't feel any different." She blinked, as if confused. "I'm this close to everything I wanted, and I don't even care as much as I thought I would."

Lycaster agreed. "It's just a pretty rock. We've been training to find a pretty rock. And we've had to dig out a dead body for it."

Janina rubbed Kamine's shoulders. "I think what they're saying is that you can have it. It's yours."

Kamine opened her mouth, but closed it again. She was ready to immediately dismiss it, and ask one of them to take it. She didn't want it. She wouldn't have survived the last few months alone, it was the work of a collective that had brought her the courage to do this.

So she wouldn't take it. At least not on her own.

"We should all have it," she said with conviction. "We take it together." Confusion danced across all of their faces, so she added, "The Gods never clarified that there can only be one winner every year, so it can't be considered cheating." She shrugged. "Let's change the game."

A mischievous smile had taken over Roz's face. "Let's do it."

The others nodded in approval. They had started this together as one cohort, and they would end it as one.

Kamine counted down as more rocks pelted down around them.

At once, they all touched the amethyst gemstone.

At once, the world around them stilled.

Twenty-One

The silence was deafening. Her ears rang with all that she accomplished with her cohort. Her fingers tingled where they made contact with the Heart, as if congratulating her. It felt both unreal and real at the same time. The Heart of the Thunder Court was gracing her skin.

"We did it!" Roz exclaimed, her face beaming with an almost disturbing delight.

The others cheered and hollered, proud of what they accomplished. Zoya was the first to let go of the Heart as she embraced Janina tightly. Lycaster fell to his knees, but all the adrenaline must have prevented him from feeling the pain of the hard ground.

Kamine's own joy was short-lived. A churning in her stomach told her something was off. A deep despair seemed to loom.

"Zoya, did you stop all the rocks?" Kamine asked.

Zoya responded, her face cringing. "It slowed when I left, but you know this doesn't end until the Heart is found. There might have been another onslaught."

Kamine furrowed her brows. Her family had to be alright. Grimot had to be alright. She tried convincing herself, but the feeling deep in her gut told her otherwise, told her she needed to run.

"I need—" she stumbled over her words. Zoya gave her an encouraging smile. "I should go," she pointed behind her.

Kamine finally let go of the amethyst Heart. The sensation of success wiped away from her, and the seriousness of it all came back. She needed to find Grimot. She needed to find *her* heart.

Even with all the training, Kamine's feet were tired. Her ankles ached, and she kept almost twisting them on the uneven ground. She wanted to get to him fast, but she also wanted to be in one piece when she arrived. One of the lenses of her glasses had cracked at some point, but she didn't let that deter her from her goal.

Grimot is okay, Grimot is okay, she chanted to herself as she pumped her legs across one village, and into the next. People began to come out of their safe havens to inspect the damage. They were barely a whisper in the wind as she trudged forward.

At one point, she was in a large empty field, and a few cattle grazed the grass. They looked spooked from the Undertaking, but hopefully some grass in their bellies would calm them.

Luckily, Grimot and Zoya came from the same village in the east, Schod, so she knew the direction of it. Though, she had no idea exactly where she was or how much farther it was to Schod. She searched for a home on the farm, and found a barn. No one was inside, but when she circled the perimeter, she found an old woman, shoulders hunched forward due to age, with her head bent upwards and yelling at the roof.

"Excuse me," Kamine said with a sense of urgency in her voice. "Do you know which way is east?"

The woman stepped back, startled. Kamine didn't notice it until now, but the woman's arm was wrapped in a sling. "It's that way," she pointed to her right with her uninjured hand.

Kamine prepared to leap off and go, but stopped herself as the woman turned her eyes back to the roof, her hand arched over her eyes to block the sun that had just come out.

Kamine took a peak and noticed a small cat perched up there. It looked frightened.

"She won't come down," the woman said. "She was out here during it all. She's lucky to still be kicking."

Kamine didn't think twice. She moved the ground beneath the barn and the cat leaped down into the woman's arms after some hesitation. Hopefully, that didn't further traumatize it.

The woman thanked her, but Kamine was off before she could finish.

Each street she passed, each hill she tiredly faced, brought her closer to him. The only thing that motivated her to continue was to see his face and the stubble that covered it. She couldn't wait to drag her fingers through his hair, couldn't wait to press her lips into his, not caring how disheveled she appeared.

She couldn't wait to tell him that she, along with the others, found and touched the Heart together. She had broken his curse because she had accomplished this with him. Without him, she never would have been able to do it.

She was ready to hear his side of his story, to listen as he explained himself. Like Zoya and Janina said, she deserved the truth—his truth, not Kestra's.

She crossed into his village and as she crept further in, the damage appeared minimal. A tree had been crushed, the roads blocked. Zoya had done a good job.

Kamine sighed a breath of relief.

Then, she heard a raging scream.

Kamine bolted in that direction. A pregnant woman was kneeling in front of what Kamine assumed was her home. A man was digging through the rubble. Kamine noticed, as she neared, his arms were slashed with red marks.

"What happened?" Kamine asked them urgently.

"He's trapped, he's trapped!" the woman shouted while she rocked back and forth on her knees, holding onto her belly, as if the life inside her could bring out the life under the rocks.

"Who?" Kamine whispered, already knowing what the response would be.

"Grimot!" the woman yelled, as if she were calling to him, and not responding to Kamine's question.

No, Kamine thought. He can't be under there. He would be dead.

"Watch out," she warned the man. Kamine now guessed they were Grimot's parents. Looking at the man now, it was obvious. Even from a distance, those piercing black eyes matched his son's.

But Grimot's father wouldn't move, as if he refused to keep trying to save his son.

"Move," Kamine said more sternly, but he still wouldn't listen. "I can help," Kamine now pleaded with his mother. "He just needs to move."

His mother nodded as she called to her husband. His father's shoulders slumped, but he finally came away from the rubble.

"I would back up and hold onto something," Kamine warned.

They seemed to trust her, and did as they were told without protest.

Kamine needed to be careful. She needed to bend the ground so the rocks on top tumbled outwards and away from where he might be crushed. So she concentrated, and she allowed the love she had for him to lead her powers. Because she did, she realized. She loved him. She had no idea when that happened, but it made sense in the end. He never gave up on her, even when she wanted him to. How could she not love him after that?

He would tell her not to, but Kamine closed her eyes. She didn't need to see the rocks moving, instead she pictured him. The way his hands were strong and confident. The way his shirt was always loosely tucked into his perfectly pressed pants. The way he had no problem wrinkling them so that he could climb on top of her, and ruin her sanity. She saw him sitting in his chair in his private library, the way he would alway lightly scratch his face as the words distracted him from the world, and how with just one word from her, she could pull him back out.

"Come back to me," she said and repeated. "Come back, come back."

The pile of rocks moved. She had no idea where his body would be, but she trusted her powers would instinctively guide her. She poured out her love in bursts. Love for him. Love for her family. Love for her mother. Love her friends and cohort.

"I see him," his father said.

Kamine opened her eyes, and she saw his body. His arm was bloodied, but she could see the small rise and fall of his chest. She let out a whimper as she went to his side, tripping over the rubble.

She touched his cheek, but his eyes remained shut.

"Rest," she whispered. "We'll get you somewhere safe."

Twenty-Two

Grimot's eyes peeled open. He didn't know where he was, but he knew he was not the same.

Heavy breathing echoed in his ears. He tried to turn to the source of the noise, but his neck twitched in pain. That's when he noticed it. His arm was gone from right where his elbow once was. White bandages were wrapped tightly around the wound.

What happened?

The last thing Grimot remembered was being in his old room with his parents stowed away somewhere safer. The next, he felt Kamine's touch on him before he went out like a light again.

"You're up," a voice croaked. Kamine stood up from a chair. There was a blanket wrapped around her shoulders. Her glasses partially concealed the dark bags under her eyes, but he could read in her posture how tired she was.

"You're here," he managed to say back.

A cry escaped her lips. He extended his one arm to her, and she fell into him. He winced, but he didn't care about the pain anymore—he only cared that she was there with him. He rubbed her back as she sobbed.

"I was so scared," she said. "I thought you were dead."

"What happened?" he repeated the question out loud this time, seeking any answers.

She pulled back and sat on the edge of the bed. She wrung her hands together, picking at a scab, her eyes downcast, barely looking at him. Not out of fear though. Something bigger than that.

"The Undertaking was successful. We all won," she shrugged casually.

He blinked, trying to make sense of that statement, but couldn't. "What does that mean?"

"It means...we beat the system. We played the Weather Gods' little game and followed their rules, and all won. We all touched the Heart at the same time."

"There have never been multiple winners." And they didn't know the consequences of what it would mean now that it had been done.

"No one in the past wanted to share the glory."

He huffed. Had it always been that simple? Grimot had a hard time believing that to be true, but he didn't want to suck the joy from her. "I'm proud of you."

"You haven't heard the best part."

"What's that?"

She beamed with pride as she said, "Now that you're alive and breathing, we can officially say that there were no casualties."

In that joy, he saw the relief that consumed her. She had been so stressed, but she set out a goal for herself, and had accomplished even more. He wanted to kiss her.

"Except your arm," Kamine corrected. "How do you feel?"

He didn't know, not yet anyways. "It's an adjustment."

He could see the guilt etched in her features, and he hated that she even considered it her fault.

"Don't blame yourself," he said with such passion, not giving her the room to doubt him. "You saved me in more ways than one. You broke my curse."

The heavy weight that consumed him for years had disappeared. When his arm had started turning to stone those seconds before it all turned black, he had accepted his fate. He would be forever lost in the dust and rubble, a punishment he deserved.

"You found me. Just like you found the Heart," he continued, when he could still see her worry. "My existence will always trace back to you, my purpose in life to be consumed by you. I'll never get lost again."

She laid down next to him, and he wrapped his arm around her. Her presence was like a balm to his soul. Just having her next to him solved so many of his worries. He knew he still had explaining to do—and that time would come, because he owed it to her. But it was a comfort to know that she still wanted him.

"I like it," she said as she brushed her finger across his chest.

"Yeah?"

"It'll be easier to tie you down." Mischief lined her voice, and he was so grateful for the light-hearted change of tone. He needed it, and she recognized that.

He snorted, "I like the way you think."

"I also like that it means I still have you, that you're still alive," she said into his chest.

"You still want me?" He felt her nod against him. "I want you, too."

"Good because I—"

He shushed her. "I want to say it first."

She scoffed as she lifted herself up to look at him. Those purple eyes were practically glowing in the light now. "So bossy," she crooned. "I'll allow it only because you lost an arm yesterday."

He pushed himself up so that he was level with her. Their lips were so close as he said, "I love you."

She pecked him on the lips. "I love you."

And those words were the beginning of every beautiful moment to come.

Epilogue

A small celebration took place in Kamine's village. Her father helped her set up tables and chairs outside for her cohort. Grimot used his one arm to lift chairs, even as her father scolded him. Kamine just chuckled.

Damien carried bundles of wildflowers that he had picked. Kamine placed them into vases, and distributed them across the various tables.

Kamine put her hands on her hips, assessing everything. Villagers had all brought forth their thanks by cooking meals that Kamine would happily share with her cohort and friends. There was a plethora of potatoes, steamed vegetables coated in butter and garlic, sausages, and more. Even with the overabundance of food, she knew that the others would eat every bit of it up after eating mushy gruel, and dry, flavorless food for months.

A hand wrapped around her waist from behind. Grimot rested his head on her shoulder.

"It looks delicious."

"They deserve it," she said.

After Kamine confirmed that Grimot was alive and well, she went back to the school the next day to pack up her things.

The others were there, too. They spent the night in one of the lounge rooms, recounting their Undertaking and everything that happened before they reached Kamine's village and found the Heart together.

Lycaster had brought too many bottles of wine that they all indulged in, and the whole occasion was relaxing and fun. The weight of her Undertaking was now lifted, but too was the weight of her resentment towards her mother. Kamine felt refreshed and light. She would never forgive the Weather Gods for forcing its people through such a tortuous event each year, but at least she now knew it was possible to change the trajectory of the game.

That was Kamine and Grimot's plan for next year, and beyond. Even handicapped, he could still perform magic, so he would continue to teach—having found a new passion for helping the newest cohort members, his purpose for teaching no longer brimmed with guilt and anger. Plus, having one less arm would only make it easier to prove how someone didn't need to use their hands to make their powers work, Grimot had explained to her as they lay in bed together one night. Kamine, on the other hand, would join as an instructor for the newly appointed strategy and teamwork class.

Kamine would hate to be trapped in the dark school for months every year, but she was willing to make that sacrifice to ensure that lives were saved. It was time to reframe how the Undertaking was viewed in the Thunder Court. It was more than just a game. Lives were at stake.

Headmaster Dritoria had loved the idea. Kestra had only said that the Weather Gods did not like to be played with. Kamine suspected that Kestra didn't like that the cohort had succeeded, and that Grimot supported Kamine. Though Grimot voiced his own concerns as well. He believed the Gods would take their revenge on the Thunder Court at some point. But for now, all was well, and Kamine wouldn't harp on what-ifs.

"You did it," he kissed her cheek.

"*We* did it," she said, pleased with everything the last months had brought her.

"They're coming," he said.

She turned her gaze over to the hill, where the group of people she would always be connected with, who would always have a piece of her heart like they had hers, came to gather together once more.

Acknowledgements

Once again, I am left in such shock that I wrote another book (or novella I should say). This journey is tough but so special at the same time. Thank you to all those that gave *Of Snow and Sapphire* a chance. I hope this one delivered, too!

I have so many people to thank for helping me get to the finish line.

Aubrey, your covers are stunning and perfectly fit my vision for this series. I am so happy to have found you and to be working together.

Des, the ability you have to transform a story into something so special is such a gift. My words are forever indebted to your mastery.

I have to thank Jess from Truly Yours PR for helping me with my ARC management for *Of Snow and Sapphire*. You made the launch of that book so wonderful and smooth. And THANK YOU to all the ARC readers who posted and reviewed. It truly was such a great day because of you.

To Lemmy from Luna Literary Management, it's been such a pleasure working with you on ARCs for this book. I love the community you have created and the work and passion you put into what you do.

I can't wait to continue on this journey. This series is such a joy to write!

About the Author

KC Silver is a born and raised Chicagoan, spending her days exploring the city, one train stop at a time. She currently works as a media planner at a large media agency where she daydreams of the day when a Slack notification no longer makes her heart jump in fear.

KC enjoys character driven stories where the main character is on a journey of discovering themselves and learning to let go of the expectations weighing on them, while falling in love.

She can be found on all socials at @bysilverstories